Mu on Matia

*A San Juan Islands Mystery
Book Three*

**By
D. W. Ulsterman**

Copyright © 2017
All rights reserved.

For my brother, Derek.
We knew these islands as boys.
I wish you were still here so we could have known them together as men.

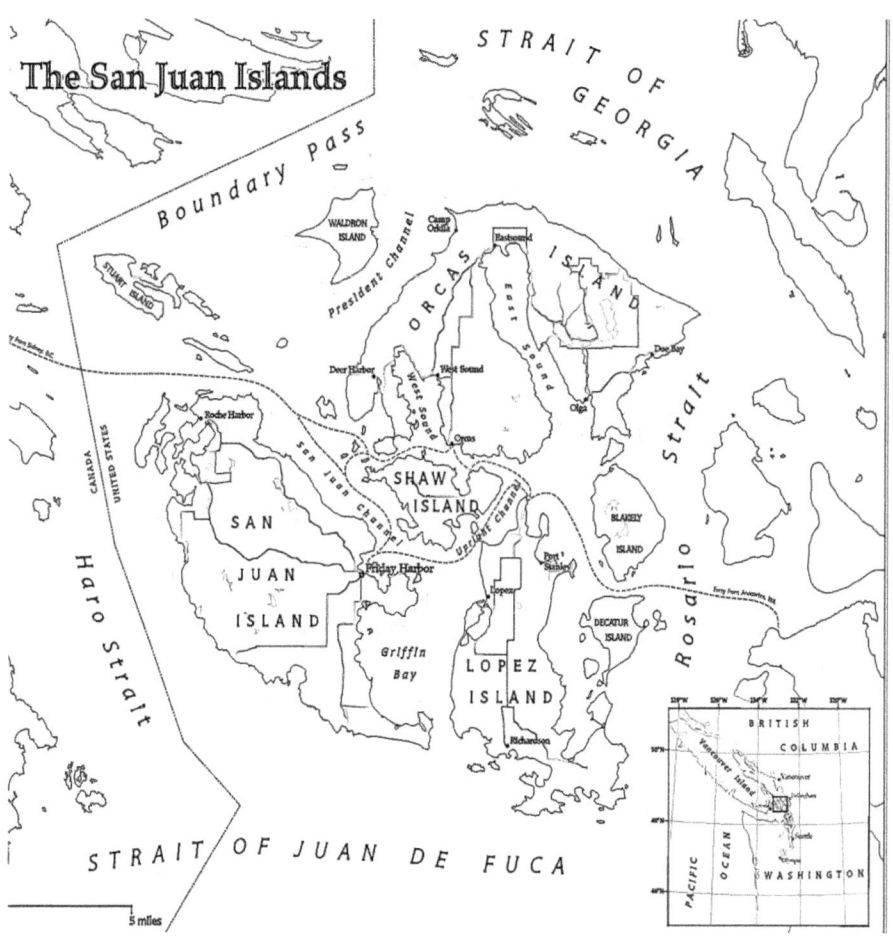

Sometimes you can only find Heaven by slowly backing away from Hell.
—Carrie Fisher

PROLOGUE

It really is true what they say—the human heart can only take so much.

That was the final, devastating lesson delivered upon forty-seven-year-old Carl Blime two days before his body was discovered by fellow island resident Bethany Bell as she kayaked alone across the early-morning winter waters of Matia Island's Rolf Cove at the northern edge of the San Juan Islands. Soon after her kayak rounded the southeastern tip of Matia, Bethany recognized Carl's aluminum skiff tied up to the narrow concrete-framed dock that extended out into the cove's protected waters.

Both had lived their entire lives in the San Juan Islands and were members of the same long-ago high school graduating class. Bethany had seen Carl fishing often over the years as she enjoyed the private solitude of her morning kayak travels. Though more acquaintances than friends, they were friendly enough that she thought to get close enough to give him a quick wave before continuing on her way, but the closer Bethany paddled to Carl's boat the more her uneasiness grew. Her eyes narrowed as she detected a dull metallic thump created by the vessel as it repeatedly hit against the dock.

Something's not right.

The little boat wasn't tied up but was being pushed into the dock by both a strong incoming tide and a slight breeze. No ropes held it in place. No plastic bumpers dangled off the side to protect the hull from damage as it hit the dock's concrete pillars.

Bethany stopped paddling and then realized she had been holding her breath for several seconds. She scanned the nearby beach, looking to see whether anyone moved about on the island's rocky shores. She saw nothing. "Carl? Are you there?"

The only answer was the distant shriek of a great horned owl from the other side of the heavily evergreen-treed island. Bethany cautiously pushed her paddles through the water a few more times until she was able to bring the kayak alongside the fishing boat's starboard side.

Carl was slumped forward far enough that his head rested facedown between his knees. He wore a dark, heavy wool jacket and blue jeans. A fishing pole lay to his right, an open tackle box to his left.

Though Bethany repeated his name once again, she already knew it was most likely Carl couldn't hear her. "Carl?"

The single word was a cautious whisper between suddenly dry lips. Bethany cleared her throat, this time shouting his name as she clung to the unlikely hope that perhaps her long-ago classmate had merely fallen asleep. "Carl!"

She moved the kayak forward until it reached the dock just in front of Carl's boat, then quickly tied up and pulled herself onto the dock with a grunt. As she stood up, she took a deep breath and then stared down at the unmoving mass that was once Carl Blime.

I have to check to see if he's really dead.

Bethany lowered herself onto her knees and reached out toward Carl's body with a trembling hand. His broad shoulder felt unusually hard, immobile, lifeless.

With gritted teeth, she held on to Carl's coat collar and pulled him upright. What she saw caused her to scream and fall backward onto the dock, then scramble away from the side of the fishing boat. The cold January air whistled its way into her lungs between tightly compressed lips.

Carl's lightly bearded face was a bloated, discolored mass of dark red and purple. At his feet was a coagulated pool of thick, inky liquid, the dried remnants of which had crusted in the stubble on his chin. Wine-red lips were drawn back and frozen in a snarl, as if at the final moment of his very last breath, Carl had realized his fate and put up a brief, albeit far-too-late struggle to prevent death from taking him.

And then there was the smell. It assaulted Bethany's senses every bit as powerfully as what she saw. It reminded her of vinegar and a hot summer outhouse.

Though the January morning temperature was barely above forty, Bethany wiped her sweating brow with the back of a badly shaking hand as she fought back the urge to vomit. It took several minutes for her to calm herself. She removed her cell phone from her coat pocket, checked to make certain she had a signal, and then dialed 911.

The dispatcher indicated Sheriff Pine would be to her location within the hour, an amount of time that seemed nearly unbearable to Bethany as she realized her only company during the interim was to be the repeated cries of the island owl and Carl's open-eyed corpse that stared, unblinking, up into the light-gray, low-hanging winter clouds that crept slowly above their heads.

By the time the sheriff's boat came into view from where Bethany stood waiting at the end of the dock, she had come to accept the shocking reality that Carl Blime was dead. What both she and the arriving sheriff didn't know was that Carl was not to be the only one.

Death wasn't finished with the islands just yet.

1

Try as she might, Adele Plank could no longer contain the happiness that demanded to be let out for all the world to see. She smiled, laughed a little, and then smiled some more.

Life was good.

Not perfect, mind you, but far better than she would have thought possible just a few months earlier. She enjoyed her work, the respect of the community she now called home, and the love of friends whom she continued to grow closer to with each passing day.

"A toast to our Adele! The single greatest journalist to ever step foot on these complicated shores."

Avery Jenkins, part owner of the newspaper where Adele worked, lifted an actual piece of lightly buttered toast into the air and held it above the small table at the newspaper's back office space. Avery's longtime wife and business partner, Bess, lightly tapped her husband's toast with her own.

"I'll second that!"

The old couple chuckled at their little joke, exchanged a quick glance, and then looked across the table at Adele's still-smiling face. Bess nibbled a corner of her toast and then leaned forward, bathing Adele in the warmth of the older woman's grateful gaze.

"We are so proud and so appreciative for what you have done with this little newspaper of ours, Adele. Ad revenues are way up. We have people reading it off the website from all over the world. It's simply remarkable, the transformation since you arrived."

Avery nodded his wizened head. The elderly newspaperman had grown even thinner since Adele had first met him last summer. His walk was now a very slow, deliberately careful shuffle since he fell over a slight rip in the office carpet a few months earlier. Thankfully, he'd escaped that fall with little more than a bad bruise. He was all too aware of the dangers posed by breaking a hip, which too often can send someone of his advanced age into the hospital, never to return.

"Bess is so right, Adele. You've saved this business she and I have built together over all these years. You've become so much more to us than just an employee. That's why we've decided to make you an equal partner."

The small plastic cup of freshly squeezed orange juice Adele held was suspended halfway on its journey from table to mouth. "What? I don't understand."

Bess gave Adele a quick smile. "It's simple enough, young lady. The time we've spent together, the care and dedication you've shown to the newspaper, it only makes sense we give you a fair share. You're part owner now. A third of the *Island Gazette* is yours. And when we're both gone—"

Adele set down her cup of juice. "Wait-wait-wait, I can't accept that. It's too soon. I've only been working here for just over six months."

Avery grunted. "At my age, six months is a *long* time, Adele. Hell, let's not kid ourselves. These days, it's a lifetime! I hardly do any of the legwork anymore, and you're getting better and better with the publishing program, so pretty soon you won't even need me for that, either. And you know, with the money the paper's making these days, financially it's a pretty good deal for someone your age."

Adele looked down at her hands, which she had folded in front of her. "It's not about the money. It's *never* been about that."

Bess reached over and placed a hand over Adele's. "We understand that, dear. That's a big part of what makes it such an easy decision for us. It's clear how much you love this business. We know you'll do right by it when we're no longer around."

Adele felt the recent smile on her face being replaced by a scowl. The thought of island life without Avery and Bess Jenkins was too painful to contemplate. With her own mother having moved to warmer temperatures in Arizona, the old couple had become family to her.

"I don't want to think about that. You two aren't going anywhere anytime soon, okay?"

Avery folded his bony arms across an equally bony chest and shrugged. The red, green, and blue wool sweater he wore had been a Christmas gift to him from Adele. "Well, knowing we were doing right by you would go a long way in relieving some of my stress, young lady. How about you agree to our making you an equal partner, and in return, I promise to do my very best to stay above ground for as long as possible?"

Bess gave Adele's hands a quick squeeze as the old woman's head nodded several times in anticipation of Adele's answer. "I'm going to hold you to that. So you agree to be a partner in the business?"

Adele sighed and then smiled. "Yes. And thank you. I couldn't ask for better business partners or better friends. You've done so much for me since I came to these islands. I love the both of you very much."

Avery sniffed and cleared his throat while looking away, not wanting to reveal to the others the tears that were forming. Bess didn't care even a little about trying to hide her emotions. She cried and laughed at the same time as she pushed up from the table and moved toward Adele with her arms outstretched. Adele stood up as well and answered Bess's hug with her own.

The brief celebration was abruptly interrupted by the blaring ring of the phone that occupied a corner of the reception desk at the office's entrance. Bess withdrew from Adele and turned to make her way toward the front office, leaving Adele and Avery alone in the back.

Avery ran a hand through what little was left of his thin white hair, and then his eyes widened slightly as he looked up at his new business partner. "Say, I was told the other day a construction crew was breaking ground down at Cattle Point. Is that true?"

Adele nodded. She had been following the story of local businessman Roland Soros's ongoing efforts to buy up large sections of property that made up the southernmost point of San Juan Island. Roland had already admitted to her months ago his intentions to build a world-class resort, entertainment complex, and casino on the location, something that would no doubt generate a great deal of animosity among some of the locals.

"Yes, Roland mentioned to me a couple weeks ago there would be someone out there doing preliminary site prep."

Avery's mouth dropped into a deep-lined frown. "Seems a bit presumptive, how he's spending money like that on such a significant project that still remains so far from county approval, don't you think? I know Mr. Soros is connected, just like I know he's spent a small fortune putting politicians in office who will do his bidding, but still, the public outcry against that project will be significant, perhaps more significant than even his money can overcome."

Adele felt her body tighten. The subject of the controversial Roland Soros remained an uncomfortable one between her and others—including Avery. Where some saw Roland as a spoiled child of wealth now obsessed with making himself even richer, she saw him as a well-intentioned though complicated man who wanted to improve the area's economy. That didn't mean Adele agreed entirely with Roland's version of community prosperity, but rather that she simply understood him better than most.

"He's been a big help in increasing the newspaper's ad revenue."

Avery's eyes narrowed. "Sure, he's spent some money on ads and likely pressured others to do the same. But don't think for a minute the single most important reason for our success hasn't been *your* reporting, Adele. Our website revenue is almost equal to the print ads, and that's from readers who don't even live here and have nothing to do with Roland's influence locally."

Adele was about to reply, but then both she and Avery turned at the sound of Bess returning from the front of the office. Bess took a moment to smooth a crease in the long, dark-green dress she wore, but Adele knew instantly it was a gesture intended to give her time to compose herself. When the old woman looked up, her eyes further confirmed Adele's suspicions that serious news was about to be delivered.

"That was Sheriff Pine on the phone. A kayaker discovered a body this morning out on Matia Island. Apparently, the deceased was Carl Blime. He was found dead, sitting alone in his boat. The sheriff said he'd have an initial statement to us for the newspaper by the end of the day. Until then, he asked to see Adele at his office to go over the initial public details of the case. He was hoping you could get there as soon as possible, Adele. I told him you were here."

Adele looked at Avery and then back at Bess. She gave a short nod, her mind quick to transition to the emerging investigative task at hand. "Did you know the deceased?"

Bess's brow furrowed. "Not well, no. He divorced his wife some years back. I believe her name was Katie. She took their two kids back to the mainland. As far as I know, he's been living alone ever since. I don't recall anyone saying an unkind word about him."

Avery shook his head, clearly saddened by the news. "He couldn't have been more than fifty. That's rather young for someone to suddenly die like that. I know it does happen from time to time. Perhaps he was ill."

After telling Avery and Bess she would update them when she knew more, Adele headed toward the front office and the door leading outside. While she knew it was possible for a man not yet fifty to suddenly die of a heart attack or some other medical emergency, having Sheriff Lucas Pine request to see her so soon in his office indicated there was likely something more to it than that.

And if things were complicated between her and Roland Soros, they were every bit as complicated between her and Lucas. She remained attracted to each of them for different reasons, while she was also determined to maintain a professional relationship with both men until such time as she could determine which one was worth the emotional risk of taking their relationship further.

In the meantime, Adele had a job to do. She was certain that would likely prove more than enough to keep both mind and body occupied.

2

"It's been a few weeks. How have you been?"

Adele's mouth formed a thin smile in response to the sheriff's attempt at small talk. She sat across from his desk in his office. "What's with the signs?"

Lucas pointed to his left where a stack of different-color political signs with his name emblazoned across them, leaned against the wall. "Oh, yeah, I'm trying to decide on a design for the election coming up next fall."

There was a brief pause in the conversation, which allowed Adele more time to note the rather sad attempt at a mustache forming over Lucas's upper lip. She tilted her head as she chuckled. "What's going on there?"

The young sheriff's hand momentarily covered the lightly whiskered space as his cheeks colored with embarrassment. "I thought it would help me to look older. It was Samantha's idea."

He was referring to Samantha Boyler, the somewhat wide-hipped, middle-aged receptionist who Adele had originally met during her first visit to the sheriff's office last summer. "Bad idea?" he asked.

Adele couldn't help but feel a little sorry over the obvious insecurity being exhibited by Lucas as he faced the prospect of an upcoming election. "It's fine. I wouldn't call it your best look, but maybe I'm a little biased. Is anyone else running?"

The sheriff leaned back in his chair as he shrugged his muscular, well-formed shoulders that appeared ready to burst from his tight-fitting, olive-colored sheriff's department uniform. "No, nothing official yet. There's been talk of Roland backing someone against me, though."

"Really? I thought you two were getting along?"

Lucas grunted. Both he and Adele knew that "getting along" was hardly an accurate term. The two men were engaged in a prolonged, unspoken truce while both vied for the affections of the same woman. "Have you spoken to him recently?"

Though he tried to make the question sound casual, Adele was well aware Lucas was fishing for information on the state of her relationship with Roland. She didn't take the bait but instead changed the subject to what she knew to be a far more important and pressing matter—that of a dead body having recently been discovered on the islands. "How about we discuss Carl Blime's passing? Do you suspect any foul play?"

Lucas sat silent for several seconds, likely considering how quickly Adele moved to change the subject once Roland's name had been mentioned. Then, just as quickly, the sheriff's tone changed as he focused on matters of law enforcement. "This is all off the record, correct? I'll have an official press release to you later today."

Adele was quick to agree. "Of course. Did you know him well? Mr. Blime?"

Lucas sat up in his chair and let out a sigh. "No, not really. I've already conducted some initial questioning of neighbors and former coworkers. He divorced his wife about seven years ago and had pretty much stuck to himself since then. Had to quit his job at the mill two years earlier because of a back injury. Nobody has seen much of him since then. He still did a little fishing from time to time, but a neighbor said even that was getting difficult due to his back pain. I just had the body sent out to Bellingham for a full autopsy report from the Whatcom

County coroner. We should have the results back within forty-eight hours."

Adele was intrigued, not so much by what the sheriff was saying but rather by what he had, to that point, chosen not to say. "You didn't answer my question about suspected foul play."

One side of Lucas's mouth pushed outward into a half smile. "That's because there was no evidence to suggest foul play, at least not *directly*."

Adele found herself leaning forward in her chair. "What does *not directly* mean?"

The sheriff opened the top drawer of his desk and removed a single, unlabeled manila file folder, which he then pushed across the desk toward Adele. "That's an emergency-response log representing a certain category of calls over the previous twelve months."

Adele opened the folder and scanned a series of dates and locations, the last one indicating a dispatch response to Matia Island earlier that morning.

"Do you see a pattern?" Lucas asked.

Adele nodded. "Yes, it started out with just one call for that category, but over the last few months, there have been seven such calls, including the one you responded to this morning. They appear to be increasing in number."

"Exactly, and if my hunch is right, the one today represents our first *confirmed* fatality."

Adele looked up from the file folder. "You believe Carl Blime's death is related to these other response calls?"

Lucas clenched his jaw as he nodded. "I do."

Adele tapped the folder with the tip of her finger. "So what's the connection between today and the other calls in this file?"

"Drugs."

Adele sat still, saying nothing, choosing to wait for Lucas to continue.

"I found a nearly empty, unmarked, plastic container of pills in Mr. Blime's possession. We're conducting tests to determine what they are and will match that up with how much the deceased had already ingested prior to his death."

"You suspect it was an overdose?"

Lucas's brow lifted slightly. "I do, and I think that unless I find out where these drugs are coming from and who's responsible for bringing them into our community, Carl Blime won't be the only one to die from them."

"You said the container was unmarked. Does that mean the drugs weren't prescribed to Mr. Blime?"

"Correct, the bottle had no markings. I checked with our local pharmacy, and they indicated the bottles didn't come from them."

Adele's eyes widened. "You've found other bottles like that before, haven't you?"

Lucas stood, moved from behind his desk, and opened the door into the hallway. "Be right back."

When he returned he promptly closed the door again and sat back down. In his hand he held two identical, unmarked, yellowish plastic pill bottles. "These were taken from two different individuals on two separate and seemingly unrelated emergency response calls just last month. Both involved nonfatal drug overdoses. One was a thirty-seven-year-old mother of two who resides on Orcas Island. The other was a fifteen-year-old-boy who lives here on San Juan Island. That makes two different medical emergencies in two different locations, both linked by the very same type of unmarked pill bottle. The mother recovered after an overnight stay at our local health clinic. The boy had to be airlifted to the hospital in Bellingham and have his stomach pumped. The doctors indicated that if he had gone an hour longer without treatment, he likely would have died. Both suffered from opiate overdoses just like all the other emergency calls detailed in that file."

Adele's brows closed together as she processed what she had just been told. "Okay, so what do you need from me?"

Lucas cleared his throat. Adele took it as a sign that he was about to say something that made him uncomfortable.

"Well, you can do what you've already proven you do better than most. Keep your eyes and ears open for any clues that might help me to find out if our island residents are in fact being threatened by some kind of illegal drug trade."

Adele held the sheriff's eyes captive in her own. "Uh-huh, and what else?"

Lucas cleared his throat again as he looked down at his desk. "Have you seen or heard anything from Roland's associate, Sergei Kozlov?"

"Really, Lucas, you're back to *that*?" Sergei Kozlov was the menacing Russian business associate who had tried to intimidate Adele last summer as she sought to solve the murder of a young female immigrant worker from Vancouver, BC. Though that murder was eventually proven to have nothing to do with either Roland Soros or Sergei Kozlov, Adele had since suspected the sheriff remained suspicious over why Roland would choose to link himself with someone who had known ties to organized crime.

Lucas's tone betrayed the first hint of anger since Adele had sat down in his office. "Don't dismiss my concerns about Roland and Sergei so easily. The fact remains Sergei is a likely criminal."

It was Adele's turn to share her own anger as she quickly moved to defend her friend. "Roland isn't a drug dealer, Lucas. Even you have to admit that it's crazy to think so. He owns property. He builds things. Why would he risk all that to sell unmarked bottles of pills to people? It's ridiculous."

Lucas pointed at Adele. "Then what about Sergei? Do you feel just as confident defending him?"

Adele wasn't intimidated by the accusation. "I have no intention of defending him. The guy is a thug. Besides, I thought after you took that unlicensed gun off him last summer you revoked his passport. He isn't allowed to travel from Vancouver to here anymore, right?"

"My jurisdiction doesn't include immigration. I can make a recommendation to revoke his travel privileges, but ultimately that's the US Customs and Border Protection's call. Sergei contested my recommendation. There was a hearing. He had his high-priced attorney there, and his travelling privileges were fully reinstated."

Adele shrugged. "Oh, I see. The border patrol didn't agree with your recommendation. Is that normal?"

"I don't know. I haven't been on the job long enough to deal with immigration issues like this. Sergei is the only one so far for whom I've tried to get his travel privileges revoked. Initially, Bob thought it would be a done deal. Then he stopped returning my calls. Just yesterday I went to his office to ask him about it personally, and he said the matter had been decided and there was no need to discuss it further."

Adele glanced through the office's only window as an arriving ferry blasted its horn, the sound causing the concrete floor under Adele's feet to vibrate. She turned her head to look again at Lucas. "Who's Bob?"

"Oh, right, you likely haven't met him yet. I was referring to Bob Tinnis. He runs the Roche Harbor Point of Entry office not far from your boat slip there in Roche Harbor. Heavy-set guy, big white mustache, usually has a scowl on his face."

Adele was now able to place a name with the armed and uniformed older man she had seen several times walking up and down the Roche Harbor marina docks during the busy summer months. "Right, I know who you're talking about. So this Bob Tinnis, he already indicated Sergei's reinstated travel status was a done deal? And you don't have any influence to make him reconsider?"

Lucas shook his head. "I'm county law enforcement. Bob is federal. Getting him to change his mind on anything is well beyond my pay grade."

"I suppose you'll be watching and waiting for Sergei to do something to give you cause to arrest him again?"

"Oh, yeah, you can count on that. And with a scumbag like him, I don't think I'll have to wait long. In the meantime, though, you keep an eye out. Be smart. You weren't exactly his favorite person last summer."

Adele was about to stand up to leave when she realized she had not yet asked about Lucas's father, Dr. Edmund Pine, the island's former and beloved longtime physician who was now in the grips of quickly worsening dementia. "How's your dad doing?"

Lucas's head dropped down until his chin nearly touched his chest. "He's hanging in there but seems to have more bad days than good. He sleeps a lot more than he used to, sometimes from morning to night. He asked about you a couple of weeks ago. He couldn't recall your name, just called you that pretty brown-haired girl with the warm eyes. He's hoping you might stop by again."

"He did? Really?"

Lucas offered up a bittersweet smile, his voice drenched in the sadness that was the result of having to watch a once strong and charismatic father now fading away into nothingness.

"Yeah. You're welcome to stop by anytime, Adele. If you catch him on one of his better days, I'm sure he'd love to see you."

Adele stood up and then watched as the sheriff did the same.

"So where are you off to?" Lucas asked.

Adele's hand hovered over the door handle. "I thought I'd pay Bob Tinnis a visit—introduce myself."

Lucas reached for the phone on his desk. "You want me to let him know you're coming?"

Adele waved away the offer. "No, I'll handle the introductions, thanks. Don't forget to send the newspaper the press release on the body found this morning."

"I'll send it out after lunch," Lucas answered. "Speaking of lunch, maybe you could stop by the house on Friday for some tea or hot chocolate? I'll even use some of those little marshmallows you like. I could make us up some sandwiches if you're hungry. Like I said, my dad would enjoy seeing you again."

There was an awkward pause before Lucas continued. "And I guess I would, too. I hear the newspaper is doing great, which doesn't surprise me one bit. You're a hell of a reporter."

Adele shrugged. "Friday for lunch, huh? Sure, that sounds great, but only under one condition."

"What condition is that?"

Adele pointed at the feeble impersonation of a mustache. "All due respect to your receptionist, but you have to shave that homeless caterpillar off your lip first."

Lucas scowled as he traced the light mustache with his fingers. Despite the scowl, Adele could see his eyes were smiling. "That's a deal. See you Friday."

3

Adele pushed through the pain in her legs and lungs. She embraced the hurt, took it in, and used it to motivate her to keep moving. The cold, dry air stung the inside of her throat as she gritted her teeth and ran up the stone steps that led back to the Roche Harbor resort. Since the end of last summer, she had taken to jogging the myriad of forest trails that bordered the resort property, enjoying the early-morning, tree-scented solitude and using that time to do a mental inventory of both the previous day and the day to come. She especially appreciated the sound of her running shoes as they hit the dirt, thumping in time to the beating of her heart, a sort of symbiotic dance of body and nature.

On this particular morning, she intended to pay a visit to Bob Tinnis at the marina's customs office. The next issue of the newspaper was all but finished. Lucas had made good on his promise to send Bess and Avery a copy of the official statement regarding the initial investigation into Carl Blime's sudden death, and that death would be the upcoming issue's front-page story.

From the top of the gently sloping grassy hill that rose on the eastern portion of the resort, Adele was able to look down upon the marina, as was her habit so often at the end of her run. She still found it remarkable how different the place was during the winter months than the far busier summer season. Nobody moved along the docks. The primary parking lot to the north was nearly empty, and no parade of boats moved into and out of the harbor.

The resort was consumed by the tone and tenor of its own solitude. It was an absence of activity Adele found comforting—a slower, more contemplative pace that she had come to happily embrace since winter's arrival. She took in a deep breath, held it, and then exhaled a plume of white vapor. She reached down to touch her toes, enjoying the sensation of feeling the muscles in the back of her legs stretching.

"Sorry to bother you, Ms. Plank."

Adele rose up, startled by the sight of a shivering Phillip Ozere, the longtime manager of Tilda Ashland's Roche Harbor Hotel. Despite the cold, Phillip wore nothing more than dark slacks and a white dress shirt with a red tie.

"Mr. Ozere, what are you doing out here?"

Phillip sniffled through a red nose that was matched by crimson-spattered cheeks. "Ms. Ashland requested I make certain you received her invitation to afternoon tea today at her residence—3:00 p.m. I know you jog by here every morning, so here I am, delivering said message."

Though Adele admired Phillip's unwavering devotion to his employer, she also felt guilty over having been the cause of the hotel manager's cold-weather discomfort. "I'll be there, Phillip. Now please get yourself back inside before you freeze to death."

Phillip gave a single, silent nod and then abruptly turned and made his way down the brick-paved path toward the hotel entrance, leaving Adele to watch his departure. It was then that her eyes detected movement along the main dock that ran down the middle of the marina. It was a group of stern-faced men, all dressed in heavy black overcoats. Adele listened to the echo of the heels of their dark, polished dress shoes striking the dock's thick wood planks.

Roland is with them.

Roland Soros was at the back, appearing to be a somewhat reluctant member of the group. His head was down, his hands stuffed into his pockets, and his normally square shoulders slumped.

Her curiosity piqued, Adele jogged down the hill toward the marina. By the time she drew near to the throng of men, they had nearly reached *Branch Office*, Roland's prized aluminum-hulled Burger yacht that was possibly the most valuable vessel in a marina dotted with multi-million-dollar boats, and certainly the most storied one, given its history and a litany of guests over many decades that included both John and Jackie Kennedy. It was while Adele had been on *Branch Office* last summer that she and Roland had shared drinks, laughter, and an almost-kiss.

Adele was about to call out Roland's name when her mouth clamped shut at the sight of Sergei Kozlov, who turned around slowly and stared directly back at her. Sergei was exactly as Adele remembered him: the shaved head, goatee, dark reptilian eyes, and cruel sneer that hinted of violence at the slightest provocation.

Though layered in two heavy sweatshirts, Adele felt her body go cold at the sight of the Russian. She hated that a man could make her feel so fearful but also understood how that fear was a warning to be heeded. The men, including both Sergei and Roland, moved into Roland's yacht and closed the door behind them, leaving Adele standing alone on the dock outside just as the first droplets of rain began to fall.

Heavy footsteps sounded behind her. Adele turned and saw an older man with a thick white mustache walking along the dock. He wore a dark-blue uniform and was making his way toward the customs office.

Bob Tinnis.

Adele gave Roland's yacht one last look and then moved to catch up to Tinnis. Hearing her approach, the customs officer whirled around, his normal scowl deepening as he realized she was there to speak to him.

"Can I help you?" His tone conveyed his annoyance over having his workday begin with an unscheduled visit.

"Officer Tinnis, my name is Adele Plank. I'm a resident here at the marina and a—"

"I know who you are. I read the newspaper. What do you want?"

Adele gave a quick smile, hoping to convince Tinnis she had no ulterior motive. "I just wanted to say hello. I've seen you coming and going here at the marina for months now and figured we should at least get to know each other by name."

Tinnis stroked each side of his handlebar mustache. Suddenly, his reticent mood was transformed as he smiled and held out a thick-fingered hand, which Adele promptly shook.

"Nice to meet you, Ms. Plank. You can just call me Bob. That's what everyone else does around here. I'm gonna make a fresh pot of coffee. Care for a cup?"

"Uh, sure, thank you," Adele stammered, momentarily caught off guard by the customs officer's whiplash-inducing change of mood.

Bob told Adele to follow him to the end of the dock where the square, single-story customs office building was located. His voice trailed behind him as he continued to speak. "Part of me loves the off-season because I have the office all to myself. We don't transfer more staff until spring, and, of course, by summer we have three of us working seven days a week in order to process all the arrivals. The problem is these last weeks of winter really start to drag. Days seem to last forever, and it gets tougher and tougher to stay awake. By afternoon, more often than not, I'm nodding off. Then again, being paid to sleep isn't so bad!"

He chuckled at his own joke as he reached out and opened the door to the customs building. He turned on a single overhead florescent light and motioned for Adele to join him inside. "I apologize for the chill. It takes about ten minutes for our little heater to warm the place up. In the meantime, have a seat. I'll get the coffee going, and you can let me know why you wanted to see me."

Three wooden chairs were lined up against the wall nearest the door. Adele sat down in one of them and watched Bob disappear behind the tall counter that was home to a large computer monitor on the opposite end of the small room. She heard him opening a cupboard and then smelled the unmistakable aroma of brewing coffee. He returned from behind the counter, pulling a chair on wheels behind him. Bob placed the chair in the middle of the room and sat down with a soft grunt.

"So is it true you inherited old Delroy's sailboat?" he asked.

Adele nodded. "Yes, he left it to me in his will. We didn't know each other long, but we became close. He was a special person."

Bob pointed to Adele. "That he was—a good man. Eccentric as hell, mind you, but a good man. I've been at this job a long time, and he never showed me anything less than total respect. So, Ms. Plank, you said you wanted to introduce yourself. We've done that. Now, how about you get to the *real* reason you wanted to speak with me."

Under the florescent lighting, Adele could see guarded suspicion lurking within the forced friendliness of the customs officer's eyes. Bob had drawn Adele inside and now intended to find out the truth behind her being there.

He's thinner than I remember seeing him during the summer, Adele thought. *Not quite nervous, either, but definitely agitated. He doesn't trust me.*

"Do you know who those men are who were making their way to Roland Soros's yacht?"

The coffee maker chirped that it was finished. Bob pushed himself out of his chair with a grimace. His first two steps toward the counter revealed a noticeable limp on his right side that hadn't been there before. It was the same hip the customs officer's holstered gun hung off of.

"Tell you what, young lady, getting old is no fun. This damn hip has been troubling me for years. They want to cut into me and put in a new one, but I say no thanks to that. Maybe after I'm retired, but not right now. Say, you take any cream or sugar?"

"No, black is fine, thank you."

Bob reemerged, carrying two coffee mugs. He handed one to Adele and then, holding the other, returned to his chair. "So, what were you saying?"

"I asked if you knew who the men were who were with Roland Soros."

Bob took a sip of his coffee and then peered at her over the brim of his cup. "I know they're from Vancouver. Beyond that, it's none of my business."

"One of them is named Sergei Kozlov. Sheriff Pine recently told me Mr. Kozlov had his travel privileges reinstated." Adele purposely ended her comment without saying more and awaited a response. Bob's eyes narrowed. He no longer attempted to hide his suspicion toward Adele.

"That's right. Look, I'm aware of your history with Mr. Kozlov. The sheriff was more than willing to share his views with me on the subject to the point of being annoying. You should know that I did everything by the book, and Kozlov's case was found not to warrant further restrictions. I have nothing else to say on the matter."

"Aren't you the least bit curious as to why Kozlov is here at the marina this morning with several other men, given his links to organized crime?"

Bob shrugged. "That's none of my business. Feel free to take those concerns up with your sheriff friend. Are you doing some kind of newspaper story, or is this visit about a personal issue you have with Mr. Kozlov?"

Adele wasn't sure whether she was being baited into a reaction, and at that point, she didn't care. She was angry and wasn't about to try and make it appear otherwise. "As you well know, Sergei Kozlov threatened me, so yeah, I have every right to have a *personal* issue with him."

Bob held up a hand. "I apologize, Ms. Plank. I meant no offense. It's like I told you, I did everything by the book. Mr. Kozlov's hearing determined he could have his travelling privileges reinstated, so his being back here on the islands is out of my hands. I'm not saying I like the guy. I was just doing my job."

Adele got up from her chair and moved to the counter, where she left her nearly full cup of coffee. "I'm glad we were able to finally meet, Mr. Tinnis. I hope if I have any further questions, you won't mind my stopping by again?"

Bob stood and gave Adele a forced smile. "I wouldn't mind that at all. Besides, it's still a free country, right? Here, let me get the door for you."

Adele noticed how Bob's earlier limp had suddenly vanished as he moved without any noticeable discomfort.

He held out his hand to once again shake Adele's. "Take care, Ms. Plank. I'm sure we'll be seeing more of each other. I'm sorry I couldn't have been more help with Mr. Kozlov, but sometimes there's only so much a person in my position can do. The law is the law."

Adele thanked Bob for the coffee, and then began to make her way back to her sailboat, replaying their conversation in her head as she did so. Something troubled her about Bob Tinnis. It was an instinctive, unsettling uncertainty—but she couldn't yet figure out what it was.

"Ah, there's the nosy little bitch."

Sergei Kozlov had announced his return.

4

Adele refused to give Sergei the pleasure of seeing her fear. Instead, she took two deliberate steps toward him. She didn't look away, nor did her voice tremble as she confronted the Russian who stood looming over her. "What do you want, Sergei?"

Sergia jutted his chin upward and licked his lips. His abnormally dark eyes gleamed with intended malice. "You want to look brave, eh? Silly little girl, you should know better."

Adele took two more steps forward and delivered a stiff-fingered poke into Sergei's chest with enough force he rocked back onto the heels of his black dress shoes. "Don't threaten me. I'm not the same person you so easily intimidated before."

The Russian's eyes widened. He raised a leather-gloved hand, his intentions clear. Adele braced for the blow while also readying herself to hit back.

"Sergei! What the hell do you think you're doing?"

Both Adele and Sergei whirled around to see Roland Soros striding toward them. When Sergei's hand remained hovering and ready to strike, Roland called out again. "I said what are you doing? Everyone else has left."

Sergei's hand descended slowly until it came to rest at his side. He glanced at Adele and then looked to Roland. "I saw her watching us and thought to say hello. Perhaps introduce her to Yuri. What do you think of *that*, Roland? Would that not be a good idea?"

Roland's jaw tightened as he stood next to Adele. "It's best you go, Sergei."

The Russian's head tilted to the side, and then he started to laugh while pointing at the island businessman. "This guy, he's funny, you know? Very, very funny. He still wants to believe he has any say in what I can do around here!" His dark gaze again settled upon Adele. His smile widened, further chilling the air around them. "You and me are going to be neighbors, newspaper girl. Roland's big boat? It belongs to us now. What do you think of that? Good, yes? You can come visit me any time. Keep me company in that big bed. Or maybe I come visit you. You'll be just a short walk away."

Adele's face snapped upward to look at Roland for confirmation of Sergei's claims. The humiliation she saw within him answered long before his words could. "What's he talking about, Roland? And who is Yuri?"

For a few seconds, Roland appeared ready to attack Sergei, so great was his anger and shame at having the news of the loss of his beloved family yacht delivered to Adele by someone Roland harbored such contempt for. Then, his shoulders slumped, his eyes briefly closed, and he let out a long, slow sigh. "It's true. I sold her to an associate of Sergei's. Yuri is Yuri Popov, the new owner."

Sergei clapped his hands together. "Ah, see! And I will use it as a vacation home when I am here on your islands." The Russian's brows lifted as his eyes lingered over Adele's compact form. "We can be such good friends, now. *Close* friends, yes?"

Adele watched as Roland's anger toward the Russian return. With fists tightly clenched at his side, he growled a warning. "That's enough, Sergei. Don't think I still don't have ways of making trouble for you. Leave her alone."

Sergei grabbed Roland by the front of his jacket and pulled him close until both men were nose to nose. "No, I don't think so. I work for Yuri, and Yuri *owns* you, so you don't threaten me. I threaten you."

Adele heard quick footsteps coming from behind her and feared it was more of Sergei's people. The calm, assured voice that accompanied those footsteps, though, brought her immediate relief.

"Mr. Kozlov, I'm going to need you to step away from Mr. Soros and make sure to keep your hands where I can see them."

Sergei bit down on his lower lip while staring into Roland's eyes. Roland in turn matched that stare with an equally hard, unblinking one. He issued the Russian a thin smile. "It's probably best you do what he says, Sergei. I don't think Sheriff Pine likes you very much."

Muttering several curse words in his native tongue, the Russian let Roland go and backed up slowly with his hands held high. "And here is the washed-up football player with a gun. Come to play tough guy for his little girlfriend! Isn't that right, Sheriff?"

Lucas pushed Sergei back several feet, making certain to place himself between the Russian and the others. "Mr. Soros has one thing right, Sergei. I don't like you very much. Now put your hands on the side of the boat right behind you."

Sergei frowned. "*What?*"

Lucas pushed on the Russian's upper back. "You heard me. I'm going to search you for a weapon. Given that I confiscated an unlicensed firearm off you just last summer, I figure I'm well within my right to do so. Hands out and feet apart—*now*."

Sergei turned around with a sneer and glared at both Adele and Roland as Lucas ran his hands along the Russian's sides, looking for weapons. Once he confirmed Sergei was unarmed Lucas stepped back and with one hand on the butt of his sidearm, motioned with the other hand for Sergei to get moving.

"Time to go, Mr. Kozlov. I believe you have some others waiting for you up in the parking lot. It'd be rude to keep them waiting much longer."

Sergei readjusted the front of his overcoat and then puffed his chest out in a show of defiance. He pointed to Adele and spoke in a heavily accented snarl. "Don't forget, we'll see each other again *real soon*, newspaper girl."

Adele was stunned by how quickly Lucas moved toward Sergei and how the muscles in his forearms rippled as he took hold of one of Sergei's wrists and easily forced the Russian's arm behind his back. The look on Sergei's face indicated the power Lucas possessed shocked him as well. The Russian inhaled sharply from the pain of having his arm twisted behind him.

Lucas leaned in close and whispered a warning into Sergei's ear. "I hear you threaten Ms. Plank one more time and I'll snap this arm in two and then arrest *you* for assault. Don't think I won't."

Lucas pulled the arm even farther back, causing Sergei to cry out. As soon as he was released, he spun around to glare at the three island residents. He rubbed his arm, moved his shoulder in small circles, and then spit a wet, mucus-tinged ball of saliva at Lucas's feet. "You attacked me, Sheriff. These people saw. I have witnesses. I am going to cause you a great deal of trouble now."

Lucas shook his head and grimaced. "Is that right, Mr. Kozlov? And who do you think around here is willing to vouch for the likes of you?"

The Russian pointed at someone the others had not yet noticed who stood farther down the dock. "*He* will. He saw what you did. He will back up my complaint."

Sergei wagged a finger and grinned. "You should not have touched me, Sheriff Pine. What is it you Americans are so fond of calling such things? Police brutality, yes?"

Lucas looked behind him at Bob Tinnis, who was clearly avoiding the sheriff's gaze. "Did you see me doing something wrong here, Officer Tinnis?"

Bob scowled, looked down at his feet, and cleared his throat. Those three gestures caused Adele's heart to sink. She knew then Bob Tinnis was about to betray Lucas.

"Well, you did grab him awful hard there, Sheriff. I can't deny that's what I just saw."

Lucas's mouth fell partly open as he realized what was happening, and what could happen should a full complaint against him proceed with a Customs and Border Protection official supporting the claims of the complainant. "Bob, you can't be serious. You know his record. You know the people he associates with. Mr. Kozlov made a threatening remark toward Ms. Plank, a woman he is likely to have threatened before."

Bob shook his head slowly. His eyes remained fixed on the ground. "I didn't hear any threat. Just saw you twisting Mr. Kozlov's arm behind his back."

Sergei snickered.

Adele glanced at Roland, struck by his silence, his refusal to come to Lucas's defense. She then looked farther down the dock at Bob Tinnis.

Something about his voice, how he's speaking, it's different than when we spoke earlier.

Lucas placed his hands on his hips and rolled his head from side to side before answering the customs officer's betrayal. "Fair enough,

Officer Tinnis. You go ahead and side with this piece of scum over me, and we'll see how it goes from there. You really think he's worth the trouble?"

Bob's head lifted as his eyes peeked out from beneath heavy lids to assess just how angry and disappointed Lucas was in him. The older man's forehead was damp, his cheeks bone-white and drained of color. Then his chin dropped to his chest once again. His reply was little more than a brief, apologetic mumble. "It's what I saw, that's all. It's nothing personal, Sheriff."

Adele's suspicion intensified. Something wasn't right. *Is he slurring his words?*

A series of angry, high-pitched cries echoed across the marina as two seagulls circled directly above where Adele stood. She and the others looked up to watch the seabirds fighting. The spectacle of the aggressive gulls was soon interrupted by a heavy thump. Adele looked around until she was finally able to locate the source of the noise.

Bob had collapsed face-first onto the dock and lay where he fell, silent and unmoving.

5

"Is he going to be okay?"

Lucas had just finished a phone conversation with a nurse at the Friday Harbor medical clinic. He appeared more confused than concerned, which left Adele wondering what he had just learned regarding Bob's condition.

"Mr. Tinnis regained consciousness on his way to the clinic, denied the medical staff permission to draw any blood for tests, and after twenty minutes of observation, chose to walk out of the clinic under his own power."

"Like he's hiding something."

Both Adele and Lucas looked at Roland. They were all seated inside Roland's yacht, surrounded by the tasteful, polished wood luxury that might soon be the property of Yuri Popov, a man Roland described to the others as Sergei's boss as well as someone Roland owed a considerable sum of money to. He refused to say how much, despite Adele's repeated attempts to have Roland further explain his dealings with the Vancouver Russians.

"Seems Bob Tinnis hasn't been the only one hiding something, right, Roland?"

Roland's eyes flashed his annoyance at the sheriff's less-than-subtle accusation. "My private business is just that—private. I'm not beholden to you or anyone else to explain what my financial situation may or may not be. I owed a large interest payment to Mr. Popov. I'm cash-poor at the moment, so the *Branch Office* was used to make that payment and buy me some more time. I told you last summer I was thinking of selling her, Adele."

"Yes, and you also told me part of you didn't want to because it was such a strong link to you grandparents. Is this a business decision of your choosing, or are those men forcing you into selling what you've already indicated is one of your most prized possessions?"

Roland leaned back on the dark leather couch inside the yacht's main living area. To his immediate right on that same couch was Lucas. Adele, who was seated opposite them, took a few seconds to study both men as they sat cloaked within the silence of their individual contemplations.

Lucas was dressed in his form-fitting sheriff's uniform, a man of sharp angles and consistently straightforward demeanor. Roland was physically smaller and impeccably dressed in a dark wool, double-breasted pea coat that complimented a personality that, though outwardly pleasant, always struck Adele as something specifically made to keep the more vulnerable interior of his emotions safely hidden away.

Roland peered over at Lucas. Adele sensed his unwillingness to further discuss his sale of the yacht with her while the sheriff remained in the room with them.

"You're the owner of the only bank on the islands, Roland. I'm pretty sure that same bank holds the mortgages on at least half the properties around here. If you've entered into some arrangement with known criminals, I'd say you're problems are greater than just losing this big old boat. What else might you be forced to sell off to those people in the future?"

Adele winced. The question was so typical of Lucas—brutally straightforward. The effect upon Roland was immediate. He abruptly stood up and pointed to the door. "Sheriff, you have work to do, right? Parking tickets, perhaps? Citing someone for littering? I'd appreciate it if you'd go ahead and show yourself out so you can get to whatever it is our tax dollars pay you for."

Lucas stood up to his full height, which allowed him to look down at Roland. The sheriff gave his fellow longtime island resident a hard smile, grabbed his coat that hung off the side of the couch, and then moved toward the door. Before opening it, he paused to look back at Adele. "Don't forget Friday."

Though Adele wasn't certain Lucas intended to twist the knife, she suspected he had.

Roland's mouth tightened. "What's Friday?"

Adele was quick to answer, wanting to get Lucas moving before the tension between the two men escalated into something beyond their shared annoyance and distrust of each other. "I'm stopping over to see Lucas's father on Friday."

Roland's eyes lingered on Adele for a moment before shifting his attention back to Lucas. "Is Dr. Pine not doing well?"

Lucas hesitated, surprised by what sounded like a genuinely concerned inquiry from Roland. "Uh, he's struggling. The dementia is getting worse."

Though still a young man, Adele knew Roland Soros had already had to deal with the repeated pain of losing several loved ones. He clearly took no pleasure in realizing Lucas was likely soon to experience that same kind of loss. "I'm sorry to hear that, Lucas. Your father has always been a valued member of these islands."

Lucas gave a half nod. Adele sensed his discomfort. *He feels bad for going after Roland like he did.*

"Hey, I'm sorry for saying what I did about you having to sell off more to those Russian fellas. You're right. That's your business. I just want you to know, if you come across anything strange or they do something you know is wrong, you can come to me, Roland. Those kinds of people, you don't mess around with them. And if I do find out you're involved in something illegal, I'll come after you just as hard as I would anyone else. You and me, we go way back, but that doesn't mean a damn thing when it comes to my job and keeping the people of these islands safe."

Roland chuckled as he sat back down on the couch. "Right back at you, Sheriff."

After Lucas left, Adele moved across the room to join Roland on the couch. He looked tired. Dark pockets had taken up residence beneath his eyes. The frown lines at the corners of his mouth appeared more pronounced. And for the first time since Adele had met him last summer, Roland Soros appeared uncertain of himself.

"Insecurity doesn't suit you."

Roland's eyes fluttered as if he had just woken from a nap. "I'm sorry?"

"What's going on, Roland? You're not yourself. You seem, I don't know, afraid of something."

"Afraid? Yeah, I suppose I am a little. I have a lot on my plate right now. It's been a rough few months trying to keep the Cattle Point project moving forward without it sinking me first. Truth is, I didn't think it would be this hard, and I sure as hell didn't think it'd cost as much as it has."

Adele partially turned so she could face Roland directly. "Are you really in some kind of trouble? Is Lucas right to be concerned about what you're doing?"

Roland's smile lacked warmth and held even less conviction. He stood up from the couch and made his way toward the yacht's entertainment center housed in a cabinet near the galley. "I'll be fine, Adele. This room had a lot of guests over the years. I can remember as a boy watching my grandparents dance together many times across this very floor. And now, by this time next week, this boat will no longer be a part of my family. It'll no longer be a part of me. I just hope the bastards take care of her. I couldn't stand to see her neglected."

Adele stood as well. She could hear the great fatigue in Roland's voice, combined with the even more uncharacteristic sadness and self-doubt. "Then maybe you shouldn't sell it. Find another way to make that payment to Yuri Popov. You're right about losing this beautiful thing that represents so many wonderful memories. It's more than a yacht. You're losing a part of yourself."

Roland shoved his hands into the front pockets of his khakis and shrugged. "If there's one thing I've learned from having lost my family and being alone to make my own way, it's that eventually all things must end. Losing *Branch Office* is just another one of those things—another ending."

A song began to play over the yacht's sound system. After a few seconds, Adele recognized Frank Sinatra singing of riding high in April, and being shot down in May. She put a hand over her mouth to stifle a laugh at the sight of Roland lifting his head back and shouting the song's main chorus as he punched the air in front of him. "That's life! That's what all the people say!"

Adele and Roland's eyes locked. With two long strides, he eliminated the space between them and pulled her close. She could feel the warmth of his body and delighted in the sensation of his breath as it caressed the space just below her ear. "I love hearing you laugh," he said.

It was such a simple statement, and yet, for reasons she was unable to entirely comprehend, those words made Adele feel equally happy and sad. Perhaps it was that contrast of emotion or an instinctive need to try and help someone so clearly in pain. Whatever the motivation for what Adele did next meant far less to her than the act itself. So, without regret, without concern over how it might complicate her immediate future, Adele brought her hand to rest behind Roland's head, lifted her mouth to his, and kissed him.

After only the briefest moment of hesitation, Roland kissed back, grateful, forceful, and hungry for more. Adele matched that hunger with yearning of her own. Soon, the two descended to the floor and were lost in pleasures both given and received.

There were no financial worries, no newspaper-related investigations, no Sergei or Yuri Popov, or accusations from Lucas. There were only the two of them, together at that time, forgetting the past, and happily neglecting unknown obligations to an uncertain future.

That is, until the act reached its inevitable conclusion and the world around them came regrettably into focus once again.

As they lay on the floor, gasping for air, with their backs propped up against the couch, a predictably uncomfortable silence invaded the yacht's interior. Even Sinatra had gone quiet.

Adele watched Roland turn his head toward her, his lips parting. She sensed the three words to come from him, and shut her eyes tight, hoping that would be enough to keep those words from being spoken.

Her eyes opened.

Roland's mouth closed.

Both knew a crisis had just been averted.

That knowing was reflected by a thin smile on his face as Roland reached out and gently took Adele's hand into his own. Their fingers intertwined just as their bodies had so recently done.

The silence persisted.

6

Two hours after leaving Roland's soon-to-be sold yacht, Adele found herself trying to avoid Tilda Ashland's penetrating stare. The longtime Roche Harbor hotel owner, resplendent in her dark-green, neck-to-ankles winter dress and long red hair, sat across the table inside her meticulously furnished, Victorian-themed private room, carefully observing her afternoon-tea guest.

"You seem different, Adele. A bit tired perhaps?"

Adele ignored the attempt to glean information of a personal nature from her. Over the past several months, she had grown wise to Tilda's ways. "I'm fine, Tilda. Thank you. The tea is very good, as always. Now, why is it you wished to see me?"

As Tilda continued to stare at her, Adele silently marveled at how it seemed time had somehow managed to avoid a direct confrontation with the imposing resort matriarch. Tilda looked no older, and her eyes were no less clear and piercing, than when Adele had first come to know her nearly two years ago.

"I didn't say you weren't fine, young lady, merely . . . *different*. As for the reason behind this afternoon's invitation, he should be arriving shortly."

Adele arched a brow as she set her teacup down. "He?"

At that very moment, a light knock was heard from outside in the hallway. Tilda rose from her chair with eyes lit by subtle mischief as she moved to open the door. "Yes, and you'll see him soon enough."

Adele turned in her chair so she could watch who was entering the room. The faint aroma of woodsy cologne filled the space, followed by a familiar voice.

Brixton Bannister stepped inside and flashed Adele a brilliant white smile. He was smooth-shaven, his salt-and-pepper hair cut short, the fur-lined, brown leather aviator jacket and blue jeans a perfect complement to the custom leather cowboy boots that adorned his feet. No longer was he the heavily bearded, scraggly haired hermit of Ripple Island Adele had first met last summer but rather Brixton Bannister, former movie star suddenly returned to the world of the living in all his leading-man glory. Adele sat immobile and wide-eyed, stunned by the remarkable transformation.

"Nice to see you again, Adele."

Even Brixton's already fascinatingly deep and precise manner of speaking had somehow managed to improve since Adele had last been in his presence. She remained unmoving, struggling to form the words that adequately represented the extent of her disbelief.

Thankfully, Tilda intervened. "I'd say he certainly cleans up well. Wouldn't you agree, Adele?"

As soon as Adele stood up, a still-smiling Brixton crossed the room and gave her a long, firm hug. When the embrace ended, Adele stepped back to once again marvel at how every detail of Brixton's appearance somehow managed improve the entirety of the presentation. *And that's exactly what it is—a presentation. It's as if he's stepped out of central casting to represent the perfect embodiment of a slightly older, Hollywood leading man.*

This in turn stirred suspicion within Adele's always-keen powers of observation. She became certain Brixton Bannister wasn't merely paying her a visit, but rather that he was there to make a request.

Tilda motioned toward the table. "Let's all sit down and have some tea. There is much to discuss."

Adele's suspicion intensified in response to Tilda's casual mention of a discussion between the three of them. She decided to try to take control before she was led too far down whatever path Tilda and Brixton's collusion intended to take her. "I don't need any more tea, Tilda. I would rather you just come out and tell me what this is all about."

Brixton's cheeks colored slightly, suggesting he was afraid he might have done something to offend Adele. Tilda, on the other hand, lifted her head as she appraised Adele with the same mischievous gleam in her eyes. The hotel owner likely had little concern over Adele's suddenly more aggressive tone. In fact, Adele thought Tilda approved of her show of strength and determination.

"Very well, let us get to the reason for our being here this afternoon." Tilda shared a quick glance with Brixton, who in turn indicated uncertainty regarding how he was to proceed.

"Uh, I don't really know how to go about explaining the, uh . . ." The words trailed off, leaving Brixton clearing his throat as he awaited further instruction.

Tilda managed to smile and sip from her tea at the same time. "It seems you are in need of a script, dear Brixton! All those years living on that little island, and you're still the actor. Perhaps you should simply give the manuscript to Adele for her to read? As you already know, she's very bright. I'm certain that will be enough to get this discussion off to a more promising beginning."

Brixton shifted in his chair, lightly scratched the side of his nose, and then nodded. "Okay, if you think that's best."

Adele watched closely as Brixton reached into his jacket and then withdrew a slightly rumpled stack of white paper held together at the top by a large metal clip. He carefully, almost lovingly, placed the paper on the table before slowly sliding it toward Adele. "What's this?" she asked.

Brixton seemed to struggle to respond, so Tilda quickly answered for him. "Read the cover page."

Adele took the stack of paper and positioned it until it sat directly in front of her. Her eyes scanned the first page and saw in dark, bold print, two typed words:

THE WRITER

And directly below that, in smaller font, was a name:

Vincent Weber

Adele quickly repeated her earlier question. "What is this?"

This time Brixton found the words. He was excited, his eyes wide, and there was an uncharacteristic nervous tremble in his voice. "*That* is the industry's next screenplay masterpiece by the brilliant Vincent Weber."

Adele unleashed a long sigh. She was tired, still emotionally preoccupied with what had happened earlier with Roland, and increasingly impatient with whatever game Brixton and Tilda were attempting to engage her in. "And who is Vincent Weber?"

Brixton licked his lips, a sign of his continued nervousness. "He is, like you, a very talented young writer who also happens to have the attention of every major studio in Hollywood. His short story/screenplay won an Oscar three years ago when he was just twenty-four. And like you, he grew up inspired by Decklan Stone's novel, *Manitoba*. He then became just as inspired by your article two summers earlier, outlining Decklan and Calista's unlikely reunion after her many years as a prisoner in that man's cellar. What you have in front of you is a copy of Vincent Weber's screenplay depicting Decklan and Calista's story, from the time of Calista's supposed death to her escape and return to her old life and love twenty-seven years later. The title for the screenplay is the same as the title of your earlier article on the subject. And people who would know have informed me that there is significant interest from various producers and studio executives. That screenplay sitting there in front of you is the source of some serious buzz."

Adele took a moment to absorb the barrage of information and the potential ramifications that it presented not only to her but also to Decklan and Calista, whom Adele had not communicated with for some time. As far as she knew, they were still travelling abroad in Europe. "Someone wants to make my article about Decklan and Calista into a movie?"

Brixton cocked his head, lifted a finger, and then lowered it. "Ah, that's not *exactly* what is happening here, Adele. This screenplay is what is likely to be made into a film. You article inspired the screenplay."

Adele's eyes narrowed. It was her first indication of how things were done in the black pit that was the entertainment industry, and she didn't care for it one bit. "I'm not sure what the significance is of something that is a direct representation of my article, or merely inspired by it, and for now, I'm not interested in discussing that with you, Brixton."

Adele then looked at Tilda, who had been waiting calmly for the question she already knew was certain to come. "And have Decklan and Calista approved this yet?"

Tilda shrugged. "That would be a question best posed to Decklan's agent in New York. I'm certain that by now a dialogue has been opened between involved parties."

"Well, nobody spoke to *me* about it."

Tilda straightened in her chair. Adele knew it was a signal the hotel owner didn't approve of her anger. "That's partly why we're here today, Adele—to let you know this project is underway so you can make certain you're involved. That is, if you choose to be. I also understand your desire to protect Decklan and Calista. It was Decklan who first invited you to our islands. They have both befriended you. I see no reason why this project would endanger your friendship with either of them."

Brixton leaned forward, clearly anxious to have Adele's approval.

Too anxious, Adele thought. "How did you come to be in possession of that manuscript, Brixton? I thought you had turned your back on Hollywood, fame, being a celebrity? Yet, here you are, appearing very eager to now go back to the same life you once told me you despised."

The actor folded one leg over the other and then did the same with his arms across his chest. "I have one or two people in the business I still trust. They kept my secret and allowed me the solitude I wanted. They send me things through Tilda, primarily scripts in the hope I will decide to act again. I've ignored those opportunities—until now."
There's the answer to why Brixton is here. Look at his hair. Adele hadn't noticed it at first, but Brixton's hair was cut in exactly the same style as Decklan Stone's. "You want to play Decklan. You want to be the writer."

Brixton made no attempt to deny it. "Yes, I do, for obvious reasons."

Adele folded her hands together on the table and leaned toward the would-be-again actor. "And why is it so obvious?"

Brixton arched a brow as he considered the question. Only after several seconds had passed did he attempt to explain. "I know what it is to live on these islands, alone, with only one's memories to keep them company. Decklan's sense of loss, his isolation, and ultimately, his desire to rejoin the world—so much of that is my own story, too."

Adele felt her earlier anger return, though this time stronger, as it included her deep feelings of loyalty toward both Decklan and Calista Stone. "You don't know about Decklan's pain, and you certainly know nothing of his love for Calista—their love for each other. You're talking to me like some Hollywood hack desperate for a paycheck. I thought better of you, Brixton. Apparently, I thought wrong."

Tilda's hand slammed the table with enough force Adele felt the impact vibrate through her chair. "That is quite enough. You are welcome to an opinion, but you are not welcome to treat my guest in this manner. It wasn't so long ago that you were the young college girl coming to *my* door seeking answers about a story she knew little about."

Adele was in a mood to give as good as she got, and so proceeded to do just that. "And are you so old you've forgotten how you treated me, then? How you intimidated me with allegations of murder against Decklan that were later proven to be false?"

Tilda looked away. Adele had done something she had not thought possible—hurt the feelings of Tilda Ashland. The hotel owner's voice was little more than a whisper when next she spoke. "That is a fair criticism, Adele. You're right. My earlier behavior toward you was deplorable and as you know I've already apologized for it. I assumed you were a better person, one unwilling to repeat that same kind of abuse against others. You owe Brixton an apology. He is only sharing his love of the art he was born to create. He feels himself capable of giving the performance of Decklan the care and respect it deserves. I think so as well."

Adele glanced at Brixton. He looked down at the table, uncomfortable with the tension between the two women in the room. "And why do either of you need *my* approval? Brixton is the one with the Hollywood contacts, not me."

Tilda sat silent, apparently waiting for Adele to form the answer to her own question.

She didn't have to wait long. "You want me to help you make sure Decklan and Calista agree to this, don't you? The movie, Brixton's involvement, that's really why you invited me here."

Brixton again deferred to Tilda, content to have her speak for the both of them. Tilda finished the last of her tea and set the cup down. "It's true. You are privileged to have the trust of both Decklan and Calista. I also thought it wise to include you as soon as possible so that you might protect your own interests in this. If the film is to be made, you should find yourself compensated financially for your contribution to that process. I have no doubt whatsoever that Decklan and Calista would agree to that."

Adele was about to respond but was interrupted by the ringing of her cell phone. She looked down to see it was Lucas calling her, and immediately her thoughts returned to the time spent earlier with Roland on his yacht. *Could this day get any more complicated?* With phone in hand, she stepped away from the table. "I need to take this."

Closing the door behind her, Adele moved into the hallway where she quickly checked to make certain no hotel guests were nearby who might overhear her conversation. Once it was confirmed the hallway was empty, she answered the call. "Hello, Roland. What's up?" As soon as she spoke the name, Adele's entire body stiffened. She was horrified by her mistake, and then just as quickly relieved to hear Lucas chuckle.

"I won't even bother to ask why you have Roland-on-the-brain. Anyway, I need to speak to you about the Matia investigation, but I don't want to do it over the phone. I'm already on my way to Roche Harbor. Can I stop by your sailboat? I can be there in about ten minutes."

Adele made sure to agree quickly, wanting to move on from just having called Lucas by the wrong name. "Yeah, I'm at the hotel right now. I'll start making my way back to the boat."

"Sounds good. See you soon." Adele reentered Tilda's room and remained standing. "I have a meeting I need to make. Let's just consider this a conversation to be continued."

Both Tilda and Brixton stood. The actor took the manuscript off the table and handed it to Adele. "When you get the time, please read it. I think you might better understand my wish to play the part of Decklan after you do. Hopefully then we might be able to meet with Mr. and Mrs. Stone so we can all further discuss the matter."

Adele gave a quick nod, wanting to get back home before Lucas arrived. "I'll read it soon. Things are a little crazy right now with work, but I'll make time."

Tilda stood shoulder to shoulder with Brixton and gave Adele another inquisitive stare. "Your meeting, does it involve the rumor of a man's body being found on Matia Island?"

Adele didn't bother wondering how Tilda had come to know of Carl Blime's death. She was already an experienced enough local reporter to realize such news had a way of moving quickly through the islands. "Actually, it does, yes."

A flash of concern drifted across Tilda's face and then lingered within her green eyes. She placed both hands on Adele's shoulders and gave them a light squeeze, a gesture Adele took as an apology for the cross words each had so recently hurled at the other. "Please be careful."

Adele was surprised by the depth of gratitude she felt for Tilda's unexpected show of concern and kindness. She could not deny feeling closer to the outwardly cold-natured hotel owner, a woman whose friendship and trust Adele had come to value more and more. "I will, Tilda. Thank you."

Seconds later Adele was swiftly moving down the hotel stairs on her way outside for the unplanned meeting with Lucas Pine. As always during business hours, Phillip Ozere stood, attired in a suit and a tie, behind the lobby desk. He watched without any hint of emotion as Adele continued her hurried departure. She waved goodbye to him right before stepping out into air that had grown far colder than it had been just an hour earlier. The sun was close to completing its descent into the west, leaving the marina enveloped in winter's late-afternoon shadow.

Adele paused outside the hotel to allow herself a moment to consider the myriad of events swirling around her. She was living a life riddled by conflict and complication both great and small, with friends and acquaintances as interesting and complex as the dynamic, ever-changing landscape that was the home of her choosing, a place where one mystery inexplicably rolled itself into the next.

    She wouldn't have it any other way.

7

Lucas arrived at Adele's sailboat mere minutes after she did. His wide shoulders filled the narrow confines of the vessel's interior as he moved to take a seat across from Adele at the small eating-nook table. The sailboat rocked from side to side as the sheriff's tall frame settled in.

"Sorry for dropping this meeting on you so suddenly," he said. "There have been a lot of developments in the case, and I wanted to keep you updated. Also, I was going to stop by the customs office while I was here to have a word with Tinnis. I tried his home, but he wasn't there and he's not answering his phone. Have you seen him?"

Adele shook her head and shivered. The boat's little portable heater hadn't yet had enough time to overcome the chill. "No, not since he collapsed. You think he might have something to do with Carl Blime's death?"

Lucas's brows collided as he was momentarily lost in his own thoughts. "I'm not sure but my gut says they're not entirely unrelated. I spoke to the nurse who treated Tinnis. She couldn't tell me everything due to medical privacy laws but indicated just enough to suggest Tinnis suffered some kind of overdose. An hour after that, I was speaking with Gordy Hitchman. He's owned the Friday Harbor pharmacy for more than thirty years and has been a good friend to my dad for most of that time. He knows about this stuff, and I trust him. He confirmed there was no record of a recent prescription for Carl Blime, either through the local pharmacy or any other legitimate pharmacy on the mainland. What he *did* indicate was that he had been filling an OxyContin prescription for Carl for nearly two years, until that prescription ran out four months ago."

Adele recalled Lucas mentioning earlier that Carl Blime having suffered some sort of back injury. "And the pills you found on Mr. Blime's body?"

Lucas took a deep breath. "Gordy confirmed they were Oxy. But that's not the most troubling part. He also said each pill represented a different dosage. They all looked the same, but you could take one pill and it would be more powerful than taking three others—all from the same bottle. He called it a drug version of Russian roulette."

"How does that happen? Pills from the same bottle but with different dosages?"

The sheriff looked outside through one of the sailboat's small portal windows as the sound of footsteps came and went. "Apparently, they are throwaways, likely from a foreign manufacturer in China or India. These pills don't meet the stringent quality-control standards for import into the United States. They are supposed to be destroyed, but Gordy says they most often end up on the black market, sold in bulk for pennies a pill, and then resold to various dealers until they end up in the hands of people like Carl Blime, who likely formed an addiction while taking legally prescribed pills and then became desperate to continue feeding that addiction by accessing the same kind of medication through other means."

Adele's mind kept replaying Lucas's use of the phrase "Russian roulette." The timing of the arrival of the men with Sergei to look over Roland's yacht prior to finalizing its sale was at best suspect, and quite possibly something much worse. "So what now?"

Lucas scratched the stubble on his chin. Adele noted the attempted mustache was already gone. "I'm still waiting for Mr. Blime's toxicology report. I just checked in with the Whatcom County coroner, and they indicated they should have it to me by tomorrow. We know he was carrying what were most likely illegally obtained OxyContin pills. If it's confirmed that's what killed him, then I'm going to classify this as a murder investigation and find out who is responsible for bringing these pills into our community. And in the meantime, I was hoping the newspaper could let people know there might be some very dangerous illegal pills being disseminated around the islands—a kind of public awareness announcement."

Both Adele and Lucas jumped at the sound of his phone going off. He remained seated as he answered the call. "This is Sheriff Pine. Oh, yes, hello Bryce. What can I do for you? Is that right? Ten minutes ago, huh? Thank you. Yeah, I can check it out myself. I don't need you there with me. No, you were right to let me know. That's what I asked you to do. Okay, you take care."

Lucas returned his phone to the inside of his jacket and then abruptly got up. "We'll talk more about this tomorrow during lunch at my place. That is, if you're still able to make it."

"Where are you going?"

"You remember that dark-blue speedboat you saw out by Ripple Island last summer? The one Sergei Kozlov was driving?"

Adele nodded. The memory of that boat remained a particularly vivid one.

"That call was from Bryce Workman," Lucas continued. "He's the county park ranger for all the islands. He spends as much time on the water around here as anyone. I asked him earlier to keep me updated on any unusual boat traffic coming into the area. He just let me know that same boat you saw last summer is tied up right now at the Matia Island dock. I figure it's worth me taking a look."

Adele straightened in her chair. "That's the same dock Carl Blime's body was found at."

Lucas zipped his jacket all the way up to the bottom of his chin, clearly wanting to stay warm and to get going. "Yeah, that's right. Seems likely to be more than just a coincidence, don't it?"

Adele stood. "Wait, you're going out there at night in *this* cold?"

Lucas's eyes flickered annoyance at being delayed. "I have a job to do, Adele. And what better time for someone to smuggle drugs into the area than when it's dark, cold, and no other boaters are out there to notice? Maybe Matia is where they make the drop. Regardless, I need to get out there and take a look. I've already told my dad's nurse to stay over at the house tonight with him."

"I'd like to come with you. I can be another set of eyes. We can *both* have a look around."

Lucas shook his head as he took a step back. "No, that won't be necessary."

Adele wouldn't allow him to so easily refuse her request. "I know it isn't necessary for *you*, Lucas. I need to get out there anyway for a follow-up story on Mr. Blime's death. I wanted to walk the dock and get some photos."

"Like you just said, it's already dark—not exactly the best conditions for taking pictures."

Adele had already grabbed the warmest article of clothing she owned. It was an old, bright-red ski jacket she bought second-hand in college when she had considered learning how to ski. She never did but still had the jacket. "C'mon, let's go."

Lucas's shrug-and-grunt combo indicated his surrender. Adele also suspected he was actually looking forward to sharing the journey to Matia Island with her, and even more grateful to have her close to him.

She was also just as certain that she felt the same.

8

"Don't get us killed, Sheriff." Adele dug her fingers into the interior top of the doorframe of Lucas's SUV as the sheriff catapulted the vehicle toward the Friday Harbor marina. She had never been one averse to speed, but Lucas's driving was proving to push the limits of her tolerance.

He looked over at Adele, noted her wide eyes and clenched jaw, and chuckled. "Hey, don't forget it was *your* idea to tag along. I don't know how long that boat will be out there. If I have any chance of catching it, we've got to move quickly."

Adele grimaced. "Fine by me as long as we get there in one piece." The flashing blue-and-red lights atop the vehicle extended long, colorful fingers onto both sides of the dark pavement. Adele's eyes could barely follow the yellow line that marked the road's borders as Lucas steered the SUV into a sharp turn. She could hear one of the front tires chirp in protest as the corner was completed and then the sheriff mashed down on the accelerator as they approached the Friday Harbor city limits.

Once they arrived at the marina, Lucas hurried outside, shut the driver door, and yelled out for Adele to do the same. "We need to go!"

The barked order annoyed Adele and made her feel like a kid being scolded by an impatient father. She shot Lucas a look that would normally have caused him to take pause and reconsider his tone but instead he merely started jogging toward the marina's main entrance while motioning with his hand for her to follow.

The wind was stronger in Friday Harbor than Roche Harbor, which in turn made the temperature feel even colder. Adele ran directly behind Lucas as his long legs moved him down the steel-frame dock plank. He turned to his right toward the marina's fuel station where the sheriff's department boat was moored. Once there he paused to stare up into the sky. Adele's eyes followed Lucas's gaze as she wondered what he might be looking at.

"What is it?"

Lucas's head pivoted from side to side and then he stepped aboard the twenty-six-foot, twin-outboard, aluminum-hulled law enforcement vessel. He gave his answer as he turned around and extended a hand to help Adele onboard. "Can't see any stars. Clouds have rolled in and with this wind picking up it'll likely make for a bumpy ride over to Matia."

Adele recalled a similar nighttime journey on water from Roche Harbor to Decklan Stone's home in Deer Harbor. That night had left her with a newfound respect for just how quickly conditions on the water could change when accompanied by a change in both weather and tide.

Lucas appeared to sense Adele's apprehension and tried to lessen it with a reassuring smile. "No worries, we'll be fine. It just might not be comfortable. If you have any loose fillings you weren't aware of, you'll find out soon enough. That is, unless you want to change your mind and stay back here."

Adele scowled. She wasn't about to be frightened away by concerns over a potentially rough ride. "You just worry about driving the boat."

That answer was enough to get Lucas moving even more quickly to start both motors and untie the boat from its moorings. He had Adele follow him into the fully enclosed cabin, then secured the door behind him while motioning to the bench seat located just left of the helm. "You can sit there."

Adele did as instructed and sat silently observing Lucas as he capably captained the boat away from the dock toward open water. Once he passed the long, dark rock breakwater that marked the marina's entrance he turned on the high-powered searchlight bolted in place near the front of the bow, using it like a car would headlamps to help light the way. After a few seconds adjusting the lamp's direction via an electronic toggle switch, his hand pulled back on the dual throttles, sending the boat's bow temporarily pointing upward as the large outboard engines emitted aggressively deep, throaty growls of fuel-drenched horsepower. Within seconds, the bow lowered as the boat came on plane and bounded across the watery chop that bordered the eastern side of San Juan Island.

Lucas's face was illuminated by the green LED glow of a GPS and radar split-screen display housed in the very center of the helm console directly above the steering wheel. He pointed to an area several miles north of their current location. He raised his voice to ensure Adele could hear him over the din of the engines. "That's Matia about sixteen nautical miles away. If we can maintain our current speed, we'll be there in little less than thirty minutes."

The vessel struck a larger wave, causing Adele to rock forward until her head nearly hit the dark-gray aluminum frame beneath the windshield. Lucas warned her to brace herself against that very thing and then proceeded to increase the boat's speed even more. Adele noted how he enjoyed the luxury of a thickly padded captain's chair that included springs in the base that helped to lessen the impact of waves pummeling the boat.

"You definitely have the better seat."

Lucas tilted his head as he glanced at Adele. "What?"

Adele cupped a hand beside her mouth. "I said you definitely have the better seat!"

He apologized by way of a quick shrug. "I know. I'm sorry about that. The county approved the boat purchase just a few months ago and I haven't had time to customize her to my liking just yet. One of the first things that needs to be done is adding another chair in here so a passenger doesn't have to be stuck sitting on that damn bench."

It was nearly twenty minutes before the boat was slammed yet again by an unusually large wave. Adele grimaced as she felt her spine compress from the impact. Lucas was about to apologize a second time when suddenly his left hand shot out to grab hold of Adele's shoulder while his other hand frantically turned the wheel to the right. Adele let out a startled cry in response to the sensation of the boat falling over onto its side. If not for the strength of Lucas's grip, she was certain to have been flung around the vessel's interior like a lifeless doll, possibly causing her serious injury.

Lucas hissed an expletive as he attempted to correct the boat's direction by spinning the wheel back to center. The engines whined, seemingly upset by the erratic maneuver. The bow plunged itself into an oncoming wave, causing a heavy sheet of water to smack against the windshield as the wipers struggled to push it away.

Adele both felt and heard an oddly heavy thump from the back of the boat. This time, Lucas didn't merely hiss an expletive but rather unleashed with full-throated gusto. *"Shit!"*

The vessel had a decidedly different mechanical tone to it than just seconds before, like a duet where only one member could actually sing in tune. Grim-faced, Lucas pushed the throttle control for the portside motor into neutral while angrily muttering three words through tightly clenched teeth. "I hit something."

Adele turned to look behind them but could see nothing beyond the back of the boat. Everything else was inky darkness on all sides.

Lucas lightly tapped the engine display with a finger. "The starboard engine is fine. We're still good. I'm guessing we lost the port engine's prop. Pretty sure we struck a partially submerged log back there that wasn't showing up on the radar. Or maybe I wasn't paying close enough attention to the display."

He peered through the windshield at a black mass that rose up from the water half a mile to the west before glancing back down at the GPS display. "That big island over there is Waldron. Another few miles and we'll be passing the northern shores of Orcas, and from there it's almost a straight shot to Matia." Lucas looked Adele up down for any sign of injury. "You okay?"

Adele nodded. "Yeah, thanks to you. You don't think we should turn back?"

Lucas kept his eyes focused on the dark watery path directly in front of him while answering. "No. We're almost to Matia already. Better to tie up there and look everything over rather than make the longer trip back to Friday Harbor." He grunted as he pointed upward. "Hey, check it out! It's really coming down now."

Adele looked up to confirm Lucas's impromptu weather report and found it didn't fully reflect the significance of the white-flaked barrage falling upon the island waters. The wet flakes were actually large and heavy enough Adele could hear them as they struck the windshield like a multitude of especially fat wet bugs. The farther north they travelled the heavier and more numerous those flakes became until it appeared they outnumbered the empty spaces between them. The world beyond the windshield was a swirling winter-white mass.

Lucas leaned forward in his chair as his eyes strained to see in front of him. Adele was first to point out the Matia dock as they rounded the southwestern corner of the small island, an area the GPS designated as Rolf Cove. The only reason she was able to spot the dock was due to the reflection strips placed around the tall pillars.

As soon as his own eyes confirmed the dock's location, Lucas switched on the vessel's emergency lights, adding a festive red-and-blue coloring to the white blanket outside. He pushed the single engine that remained to the limits of its available power. "If there's someone there I don't want to give them any time to react."

Within seconds they both realized the dock was empty. Lucas used the searchlight to look down the full length of the dock to the beach and the heavily forested hillside beyond, though the increasing snowfall made it difficult to see more than a few yards in front of them. "Nothing."

Adele noted the disappointment in Lucas's voice. She watched him carefully as he sat quietly contemplating his next move. There was an inward calm to him that further magnified the natural appeal of his good looks, an indication that his physical strength was complimented by a still-developing emotional strength as well.

"This place makes sense for a drop," he said. "It has a full dock, easy access, and direct passage back into Canadian waters. During the winter months, there's hardly anyone out here, especially at night. If I were smuggling drugs across the border, this location would definitely be a prime spot to do it."

Lucas went silent again. Adele kept quiet as well, not wanting to interrupt his thought process. With the engine quietly burbling water behind them as they drifted slowly toward the dock, he folded his arms across his chest and then swiveled in his seat to face Adele. "You up for a stakeout?"

Not waiting for a response, Lucas quickly explained his reasons for the proposal. "I want to have a look at the port engine and the hull before heading back but would rather do that during the day. If this is actually a drop spot, maybe we get lucky and catch someone heading in here. If not, we get up first thing in the morning, you can take your photos for the newspaper, and I get a better look around. That's a lot of birds we get to take care of with just one stone."

"You mean we sleep here on the boat?"

Lucas gave a why-not shrug. "Yeah, I figure you're used to that by now."

Adele took the statement as an accusation and both looked and sounded far more shocked than she intended, fearing Lucas might somehow know of her recent tryst with Roland. "What's *that* supposed to mean?"

Lucas's face tightened, indicating his confusion over Adele's sudden anger. "It means you live on a sailboat. I assume that also means you sleep there."

Adele realized her error, and instantly felt foolish for her overreaction. *Smooth, Adele, real smooth.*

Lucas went on to assure her the accommodations, though sparse, would be acceptable by explaining how the boat was already outfitted with supplies intended to allow for brief overnight stays. There was a portable mattress, blankets, a propane-powered heater, an unopened box of granola bars, and a dozen bottles of water. "You get the bed, I sleep in the chair, and for dinner, only the very best—chocolate chip granola bars."

"You sure know how to impress a girl, don't you, Sheriff?"

Lucas pretended to tip the brim of a nonexistent hat on his head. "That I do, ma'am. That I do."

Soon, Adele was comfortably warm underneath a blanket as she lay atop the air mattress prepared for her. They had each quieted their growling stomachs with a couple of granola bars and water and now waited for sleep to take them.

Lucas sat on the chair with his legs stretched out and resting over the passenger bench. Like Adele, he was wrapped in a blanket. The cabin was kept reasonably warm by the propane heater that quietly hissed on its lowest setting. Outside, the snow continued to fall. Each flake was an icy whisper that gently attached itself to the exterior of the boat.

Adele closed her eyes and surrendered to the gentle lullaby of snowflakes and water. Her mind drifted aimlessly, replaying disjointed memories and thoughts as the world outside of her encroaching sleep grew more distant, less important, and inconsequential.

I'm sleeping tied up to the same dock Carl Blime took his last breath.

Adele's eyes flew open, taking several seconds to adjust to the darkness. When they finally did, she realized Lucas was also awake and staring down at her.

His low, soothing voice seemed to wrap around her almost as warmly as the blanket covering her body. "Everything okay?"

For the briefest of moments Adele considered telling him about what happened between Roland and her on the yacht. Whether it was due to fear, shame, guilt, or simply a sense the timing wasn't right for such a disclosure, it didn't matter. Adele lost her courage. She pushed away the idea in favor of continuing to keep it a secret, and instead gave the sheriff a smiling nod.

"Yeah, I'm fine. Good night, Lucas."

What followed was a pregnant pause between them. Not quite so long as to be uncomfortable—but close. When Lucas replied he sounded as if he did so from a far greater distance than the arm's length of dark space that separated them.

"Good night, Adele."

9

Dad and Mom are up. I can smell the coffee brewing.

As a child that was often the first waking thought Adele would have. She would remain in bed enjoying the warmth under the covers and listening to her parents' voices travel from the kitchen to her bedroom as they discussed whatever plans they intended for that particular day. She recalled how certain it seemed that those safe, responsibility-free mornings would continue to arrive, one after the other, forever and ever.

Now, her father was gone, and her mother was an increasingly periodic, brief, and fading conversation in the midst of Adele's ongoing journey that was her own life. Time was pushing her forward. She had come to understand that nobody, regardless of how strong or determined they were, could ever succeed in pushing time back.

Lucas is up. I can smell the coffee brewing.

Adele struggled against the blanket to sit up, craned her head to look through the boat's side windows, and saw Lucas outside with his back to her standing over a small propane burner on top of which sat a metallic coffee pot that was gurgling away. Adele brought out her phone to check the time. It was nearly eight in the morning.

After stretching her arms upward toward the ceiling, she pushed herself off the mattress and stood, surprised by how good she felt, the result of a particularly deep and satisfying sleep.

My goodness, will you look at that!

Matia Island's crown of evergreens was blanketed in a thick white mantle of powder. Nearly half a foot of snow covered the dock, with the exception of a small area Lucas had cleared off near the boat.

Adele put on her jacket and stepped outside, finding the air slightly warmer than it had been the night before. A heavy, gray cloud cover continued to hover over the islands, hinting at the possibility of yet more snow to come. The snowfall lent additional complexity to the already distinctive scent of saltwater and trees so unique to the San Juan Islands.

"Look at you, Mr. Coffee."

Lucas turned and smiled. It was such a simple gesture, yet it left Adele momentarily frozen, unable to move as she processed how undeniably attractive he was in all his coffee-making simplicity.

"Hey, I know you see me as just some island country hick, but a morning without coffee is too uncivilized to be acceptable, am I right?"

Adele found herself laughing a bit more loudly than the comment likely deserved. "Yeah, I guess so. I don't see you as a country hick, though. There's a lot more to you than that, Lucas Pine."

Lucas stood up to his full height while nodding his head in mock seriousness. "Oh, I know. I mean, just *look* at me. I'm one handsome, sexy-hot body, gun-toting badass. These days, guys like me are getting hard to come by. I guess you could say we're sort of an endangered species, which makes us rare and very valuable."

Adele looked him up and down and then raised a brow. "Well, listen to you, thinking so highly of yourself!"

"It isn't bragging as long as it's the truth."

"Careful, Lucas. That head of yours might get so big you'll topple over into the water there and I might not want to bother trying to pull you out."

"Ms. Plank, are you saying I should just shut up and pour the coffee?"

Adele struggled not to laugh as she tried to maintain her pretend criticism. "Sheriff Pine, shut up and pour the coffee."

Lucas was quick to do just that, pouring two cups and handing one to Adele. They stood side by side on the dock, quietly admiring the island's newly arrived winter wonderland, a mix of white and green, sand and stone. Two hawks slowly circled high above, their outstretched wings allowing them to glide effortlessly upon the soft breeze from the north that moved across the islands.

Adele took another sip of Lucas's dockside coffee and realized it was the most enjoyable cup of coffee she had ever had. It wasn't the flavor but more importantly the experience, the surroundings, and the man she was happy to share that moment and those surroundings with.

"I'm going to take a walk, have a look around," Lucas said. "You want to join me? There are bathrooms at the end of the dock if you need to use one."

"Actually, I do. Thanks."

They walked together down the dock, careful not to slip. Both appeared to enjoy the soft crunch-crunch noises made by their shoes as they left side-by-side pairs of footsteps in the snow. Each of them took a moment to use the bathroom and then spent nearly an hour exploring the beach and walking a narrow trail that dissected the tall trees and led to the small island's highest peak nearly two hundred feet above the water. When they reached the top, Adele marveled at the expansive islands-and-water view that stretched out before her. Lucas pointed to the east at what appeared to be a dark, weather-roughened set of giant fingers reaching out toward Matia.

"That's Sucia Island over there. And if you look north, there's Boundary Bay, with White Rock to the right and Point Roberts to the left. Beyond that is Vancouver, B.C. If it was a clear day, we'd be able to see the Canadian Coastal Mountains from here."

Adele brought her phone out and took several pictures of the dock below and the water and islands beyond. "I take it you've stood up here looking out at this view before?"

Lucas nodded. Adele detected a hint of sad remembrance as he did so. "Yeah, my parents loved this place. We would stop by here after fishing for Ling Cod over at Sucia. My mom would pack some sandwiches for us and we'd hike up here and have a little afternoon snack before taking the boat back to Friday Harbor. Once I was a teenager and could take the boat out by myself, I'd sit up here in the summer and watch all the boat traffic and wonder what kinds of lives were passing by beneath me on the water, making up stories about where those people had been and where they might be going."

Adele playfully nudged the sheriff with her elbow. "Am I the first girl you brought up here?"

"Uh, no, but you're definitely the most recent."

Adele rolled her eyes and then turned her head toward a rustling sound coming from a large thicket to her left. Lucas heard it as well and did the same.

A brilliant-colored red fox sat no more than forty feet away, looking back at them.

Lucas's eyes widened and his mouth fell open, a combination that made him briefly appear much younger than his years.

"What is it?" Adele asked.

Lucas remained quiet.

Adele glanced back at the fox and then looked up at Lucas and realized he was fighting back tears. "Lucas, what's wrong?"

He wiped at the corners of his eyes and cleared his throat. "Nothing is wrong. My mother used to take pieces of her sandwich and feed a fox that looked just like that one when we came here. It became this routine she did year after year. And I would watch my dad watching her while she fed the fox. He always had this sort of faraway smile on his face and even as a kid I understood that is what real love looks like. It didn't shout; it didn't need to. It was just this quiet little moment where nothing was spoken out loud but everything that ever needed to be said between them, was. The only time I ever saw the fox here was with my mom. After she died, we never saw it again—until today."

It was Adele's turn to fight off her own tears. The fox tilted its tufted ears forward, appearing more curious than fearful of the two humans who stood so still and quiet nearby. Adele felt something in her coat pocket, pulled it out, and looked down to see a chunk of granola bar. She took a slow, cautious step forward and held the piece in front of her. She then gently tossed it toward the fox, stepped back, and watched and waited with Lucas to see what might happen next.

The fox lowered its nose to the ground, sniffing at the nearby granola bar. With one last, careful look toward Adele and Lucas, it darted forward, took the food into its mouth, and with a final flash of red fur, just as quickly disappeared back into the thicket.

It was at that very moment Lucas's cell phone shattered the island's pristine, technology-free solitude. Adele watched as he brought the phone to his ear. He turned around, took several steps down the path and then stopped. His voice was too low for Adele to hear what was said, but the tone was unmistakable.

Lucas was being given terrible news.

With his back still to her he returned the phone to his coat pocket, took an especially long, deep breath, and then looked up at the sky above where the two hawks they had watched earlier, continued to circle above them.

Adele remained standing alone several feet behind Lucas, giving him the time he needed to deliver news she already suspected. That wait took several minutes. When Lucas finally spoke, it was with a voice cracking under the terrible burden of despair, the sound of loss, regret, and guilt.

"My dad died."

10

Adele sat inside her sailboat replaying in her mind the late-morning journey back from Matia to Roche Harbor. The water had been unusually calm, matching the stone-faced silence of Lucas as he sat at the helm, staring out through the windshield. It was obvious to Adele the sheriff was deep in thought, lost in the collective memories of a loved one suddenly gone.

It wasn't until they neared the entrance to Roche Harbor that Lucas finally looked over at Adele and mustered a thin, pained smile. "I'm okay. In fact, what is bothering me the most right now is the sense of relief I have. Isn't that terrible? I'm actually sitting here thankful my dad passed away before nothing of him was left but a drooling shell of the man he used to be. I know he didn't want anyone to see him like that, especially not me."

Adele didn't immediately know how to respond with words to such an admission. Instead, she reached out and gently rubbed Lucas's shoulder.

He looked down at her again and repeated his earlier assurance. "I'm going to be fine, Adele, really. I'm glad you were there with me when I received the news. I'm not sure why, exactly, but that meant a lot to me."

Adele asked whether he wanted her to be with him when he returned home where the body of his father still remained. Lucas gave a brief frown and shake of his head. "No, that's not necessary. You take some time to clean up, get some rest, whatever you need to do. I'll call you later."

As Lucas made the turn into the marina, the sun broke through the cloud cover for the first time that morning, creating a myriad of multicolored flashes across the harbor waters. It was a dance of a million diamonds shimmering playfully atop the small waves, as if Roche Harbor itself were attempting to comfort Lucas during his time of grief.

Adele's eyes widened as a large white-and-gray seagull suddenly came to rest on the vessel's bow railing. The seabird stared directly into the boat's interior. Its dark eyes flickered as it cocked its head from side to side, appearing to focus primarily on Lucas.

"Huh," he said. Maybe the old man was right after all."

Adele's eyes darted from seagull to Lucas, confused by the wide smile on his face that had appeared just as suddenly as the seagull's arrival. "What is it?"

Lucas pointed to the gull. "When I was a boy, I remember coming back from crabbing with my dad late in the day during the summer. It was just him and me. The sun had almost set. It was so dark we had to watch the lights from shore to guide us back. There was no GPS back then. You learned your way around the islands through experience, memory, and feel. It was just a small skiff with an old smoky, coughing-and-sputtering, two-stroke outboard hanging off the back. I sat on the bench next to my dad as he steered us toward Friday Harbor with a couple full crab pots stacked up on the bow. It had been a good day: a boy and his dad, dropping the pots, bobbing around on the water, and pulling them back up. The kind of thing so many kids today don't seem to want to do anymore. If something doesn't exist on their phones, it's like it doesn't exist at all."

The seagull adjusted its wings, dipped its head, and then continued to stare at Lucas.

"We had almost reached Friday Harbor when this seagull appears out of the darkness and lands on the skiff's bow and just sits there, looking at us. It actually kind of spooked me a bit. My dad gives me this little hug to reassure me and explains how sailors from the Old World, places like Ireland and Scotland, believed that a lone seagull on the bow of a ship that is underway is actually the soul of a loved one saying a final goodbye, telling family and friends not to grieve too much. To carry on and live out as best they can what remained of their own lives. I thought he was telling me a fib, but Dad nodded his head as he gave me another hug and said it was true."

Lucas turned the wheel as he skillfully navigated the boat around one of the harbor piers on his way toward the fuel dock. The seagull remained perched on the bow, seemingly unconcerned with how the boat tipped slightly to the right during the maneuver.

"When we finally got home that night Mom was waiting at the front door. To this day, even after all these years, I can recall so clearly the sadness in her eyes as she told my dad his father had died of a heart attack earlier that afternoon. I never forgot seeing the seagull, my dad's story of what it meant, and then learning of my grandfather's death. Maybe it was just coincidence. Or maybe it was something else."

In that brief moment between the end of Lucas's story and the boat bumping up against the fuel dock, the feathered passenger on the bow lifted its head skyward and unleashed a forlorn cry, took one final look at Lucas and then spread its wings and flew off into the winter sun.

Adele watched Lucas's departure from the dock. He turned around just once to wave at her before throttling up the boat's one remaining motor. Soon he was out of sight and on his way back to Friday Harbor. Upon returning to her sailboat, she made herself some scrambled eggs, brushed her teeth, changed into a fresh set of clothes, and then sat down at the eating-nook table where she had left the manuscript Brixton Bannister gave to her earlier. She pulled the stack of papers toward her and glanced down at the title page.

THE WRITER

Adele shoved the manuscript to the far corner of the little table. She was in no mood for reading. Instead, her mind ran circles around the subjects of the just-deceased Dr. Pine, the ongoing investigation into Carl Blime's death, and the possibility of having Sergei staying on Roland's yacht just a short walk from her own sailboat slip.

Oh, and don't forget, I have no idea what will happen with Roland Soros. Does he expect something more after we had sex? Should I want him to expect more?

Adele put on her jacket and prepared to go back outside. She needed to talk over things with someone she trusted to keep the secrets of others private.

Tilda.

The air had warmed considerably since morning, even as heavy clouds once again blotted out the sun. Adele thought it smelled of imminent rain. Nearly all the snow on the docks had already melted away by the time she began to make her way to Tilda's hotel. She had not yet walked twenty paces when she saw the slope-shouldered form of Bob Tinnis coming toward her. It was just a few seconds later that he saw Adele as well and stopped to glare back at her.

"Is there something you want, Ms. Plank?"

Adele initially ignored the question. All of her attention was focused on the painful-looking black-and-purple swelling that covered most of the customs official's left eye.

"Were you in an accident?"

Bob turned his face away from Adele, trying to hide the injury. "I'm fine."

"You don't look fine," Adele replied. "What happened?"

Bob began moving again, mumbling something about it being nobody's business. He brushed up against Adele's shoulder with enough force she was pushed sideways. She continued to watch him, noting how quickly he walked, absent the on-again-off-again limp she had seen Bob struggle with the first time they met. Adele was convinced something wasn't right about him and intended to make a point of finding out what that was in the coming days.

Before she could resume her walk to the hotel, her phone rang. She looked down to see it was the newspaper office. She took the call and was immediately greeted by Bess Jenkins.

"Adele, did you hear about Dr. Pine's passing?"

"Yes, I was with Lucas when he was told about it. He's probably just getting back home now."

Bess's voice resonated with surprise. "Oh, he wasn't at home? I didn't know that. You two were together?"

Adele went on to explain the trip to Matia, the morning walk, and subsequent phone call to Lucas informing him of his father's death. Bess replied with assurances she would handle publishing the obituary and that she had not yet heard anything regarding a public service. But she was certain information would be forthcoming soon enough.

"I'll stop in at the office tomorrow morning to give Avery the photos I took of Matia for the Carl Blime story."

Bess inhaled sharply. "Oh! With the news about Dr. Pine, I almost forgot."

Adele adjusted the phone against her ear, wanting to make sure she could hear the older woman's explanation. "Forgot what?"

"It's a terrible thing. Avery heard about it not ten minutes before we learned of the doctor's passing. A young girl living on Orcas Island, just fifteen years old, was found dead in bed by her parents this morning. We're still trying to learn more. Of course, we don't want to bother the sheriff with questions about it just yet."

Adele thanked Bess for the information and ended the call, stunned by the news of yet another death in the islands and wondering whether it was linked to the illegal drugs Lucas feared were pouring into the area. *If that girl died from those drugs, Lucas is going to take it very hard. He'll feel responsible.*

A gust of wind blew across the marina. What had been merely white clouds overhead had quickly grown darker and more ominous. Although the temperature remained warmer than it was the day before, Adele felt a shiver course through her body. Her phone vibrated inside her pocket. It was a text from Roland.

Can we talk? —R

She didn't message back, having no idea what to say to Roland. Instead, she continued on her way to the hotel and wasn't surprised to see Tilda already standing outside her room on the second-floor balcony, watching Adele's progress.

"I need to talk with you," Adele said.

Tilda gripped the balcony railing with her hands, leaned forward, and smiled. "Given the look in your eyes, I would agree. Come on in and tell me what's bothering you. I'll have Phillip prepare us some tea."

Another blast of wind pushed Adele from behind, as if Mother Nature wanted her to hurry up and get inside. The long branches of the tall evergreen trees that dominated the resort's landscape groaned their collective discontent at having their slumber disturbed by the suddenly volatile air.

Adele turned to look down at the marina. The sailboat masts were beginning to sway from side to side as water slapped against their hulls with increased aggression. A mass of seagulls flying overhead repeatedly called out urgent warnings to their feathered cousins.

It was the not-so-quiet calm before the real storm that was yet to come.

11

As soon as Tilda Ashland understood the nature of Adele's visit, namely that it would focus primarily on the subject of men and relationships, she set aside the freshly made tea in favor of a bottle of twelve-year Chivas she had Phillip promptly deliver up to her room from downstairs. Tilda poured the whiskey into two glasses, placed one in front of Adele, and then held the other over the table.

"I propose an afternoon toast to new friends discussing the age-old riddle that is love, sex, and the mess that so often resides between those two things."

The two women tipped their glasses together. Tilda took a small sip, followed by Adele doing the same. "This situation of yours," Tilda said, "does it involve more than one man?"

Adele set her glass down on the table, sensing how much Tilda was amused by her hesitation to further reveal her increasingly complicated relationships with two very different types of men. "You seem to be enjoying this far too much."

"You didn't allow me to finish. I meant to say, does it involve more than one man—*at the same time*? That, of course, is an entirely different sort of complication, but luckily for you, one I do happen to have some experience with."

Adele's mouth dropped open, which in turn elicited raucous laughter from Tilda, whose head fell back as she clapped her hands together. "Oh, my goodness, the look on your face! I'm sorry, I couldn't resist. Forgive me."

Adele emptied the contents of her glass and then slammed it down onto the table and demanded more. "Fill it up, old woman."

Tilda obliged while her hand shook from ongoing fits of giggling as she poured. "It's been a very long time since I laughed like this. Again, I didn't mean to do so at your expense, Adele. Please, go ahead and explain your boy troubles to me. I promise to play the part of the sympathetic ear, hopefully with enough wisdom to offer you some reasonably sound advice."

Adele swirled the Chivas in her glass. "Did you hear about Dr. Pine?"

Tilda nodded. "Yes. A good man. A long life. Please let the sheriff know he's in my thoughts."

"I will."

Tilda's brows arched. "Let's start with your feelings for Lucas Pine. Do you love him?"

The abrupt question caught Adele unprepared. Her eyes fluttered as she stammered a response. "What? No! I mean, I don't know. I'm still getting to know him. We're still getting to know each other."

Tilda reached across the table and gave Adele's hand a quick squeeze.

"Good! That's exactly what you should be saying at this point because you're absolutely right. You and our young sheriff don't yet know each other well enough to complicate matters with thoughts of love. There might very well be potential for love to develop, but that takes time. With that said, if you already know this, what's the problem?"

Adele shifted in her seat and cleared her throat. When she spoke, the words were a barely audible mumble. "I slept with Roland Soros."

Tilda's eyes narrowed as she cocked her head. "What did you say?"

Adele sighed, hating how her admission made her suddenly feel like a much cheaper version of herself. "I said I slept with Roland Soros."

"Why, you little slut!"

Adele blushed as Tilda's laughter once again filled the room. Soon, Adele joined her in that laughter, finally feeling comfortable enough to realize the humor Tilda's comment intended. The hotel owner blotted at the tears in her eyes and then refilled each of their glasses.

"Okay, so you slept with Roland. Knowing that, I'll simply repeat my earlier question to you. What's the problem? I assume you're taking precautions like birth control?" Before Adele could reply, Tilda continued. "You're not dating the sheriff, right? There has been no pact between you to indicate exclusivity, correct?"

Adele took another drink of whiskey, enjoying the sensation of warmth as it made the journey from throat to stomach. "No, but I'm pretty sure he has strong feelings for me. And yes, I'm on birth control."

Tilda closed her eyes and grunted. "Feelings? What do feelings have to do with this? Dear girl, at this point you aren't even sure what feelings are real versus those that actually are no deeper than a parking-lot puddle. I say this from experience. Do you really believe a man who looks like Lucas Pine, with all the likely opportunities his appearance presents to him, has been celibate since your arrival to our islands?"

Adele scowled. "That seems unlikely. Like you said, we haven't been dating."

Tilda jutted her chin upward. "Exactly. So, if you are willing to allow him the right to be a single man and enjoy the occasional romp with another woman, why don't you feel yourself worthy of Lucas giving *you* that same consideration? He has no right to judge you for such a thing, nor should you be so seemingly determined to judge yourself. It's sex, Adele. It doesn't have to be anything more than that. You're an attractive woman. More importantly, you are an intelligent one. There is no sin in enjoying the benefits of being young, single, and out in the world."

"It's not that simple. I don't want to hurt either of their feelings. I care about them both. It's why I pushed them away last summer and told them I didn't have time for a relationship."

Tilda shook her head. "That's partly my point. You're not in a relationship with either Roland or Lucas. Neither one of them has any right to dictate what you choose to do with them or anyone else. You slept with Roland. *So what*! You can't be responsible for how Lucas might feel about that any more than you would have a right to judge him for someone he had been with."

"And what about Roland? What if he thinks we're in a relationship now? He just messaged me, asking to talk."

Tilda pursed her lips. "You poor thing. You seem so willing to undermine your own right to self-determination regarding the matter. Listen to me. In this life you must focus on your own choices and not be so concerned with how others may or may not react. What Roland thinks or doesn't think is irrelevant. It's what *you* think that actually matters. You slept with him. If you want to just remain friends, then that is what you do. And if you wish to pursue something more meaningful with Lucas, then *that* is what you do. If either man has a problem with you making your own choices, then you tell them to go to hell and move on. Live your own life. Don't try and find your own self-worth from the approval of others. That is a path that will only lead to perpetual unhappiness."

With Adele's Roland and Lucas dilemma explained and Tilda's advice on that subject concluded, the conversation turned to matters of Adele's work. Tilda expressed considerable interest in the ongoing investigation into Carl Blime's death, the sale of Roland's yacht to the Russians, and Sergei Kozlov's leering threat to become Adele's neighbor.

"Have you had a chance yet to read any of the manuscript Brixton left with you?"

Adele tried not to feel guilty per Tilda's just spoken advice but failed. "No, not yet. I will soon. I promise."

Tilda shrugged. "I know you will. I'm not worried. What I am looking forward to is hearing your thoughts on the screenplay. I understand your plate is quite full at the moment. I can wait."

"What about Brixton? Is he willing to wait as well?"

Tilda chuckled. "Ah, that one has reawakened the actor in himself. He's likely not nearly so patient. I must admit it's interesting to see him so engaged in something again."

Adele thought to ask Tilda a question, changed her mind, and then changed her mind again.

Tilda's eyes narrowed. "Go on. Ask me whatever it is that has you suddenly so quiet."

The sound of a hotel guest's footsteps echoed in the hallway outside the room.

"Why are you so interested in helping Brixton? Does it go beyond just wanting to see him acting again?"

"I've known Brixton for many years. Even when I was at my worst, lost in my mistaken anger toward Decklan Stone, Brixton didn't judge. He didn't try to change me or think himself my better. He would simply show up here at the hotel from time to time, face hidden in that mass of beard, clothes hanging off him, smelling of salt and sweat, merely grateful to have a moment of my time. That is loyalty, and loyalty has *always* meant a great deal to me."

It was Adele's turn to push Tilda on her true motivations for the actor. "Let me try to be more specific. What I want to know is do you have feelings for him?"

Tilda stood and walked toward the window where she stood looking out at the darkening skies. "That's a different topic of conversation perhaps better suited for another time."

Adele was about to press Tilda further on the subject but changed her mind when she saw Tilda's body stiffen as she leaned forward until the tip of her nose pressed against the window glass. Then she recoiled with a loud gasp.

"What is it?" Adele asked.

With panic etched across her face, Tilda ran into the hallway, shouting for Phillip. Adele moved toward the window and immediately saw the roiling black clouds coming from the far corner of the marina along with the various shades of yellow, orange, and red. Like Tilda, Adele gasped as well. She blinked several times, hoping her eyes were mistaken, but the unfolding destruction outside remained.

Roland's beloved yacht was engulfed in flames.

12

It was a late, rain-drenched evening that found Roland Soros still standing on the dock staring out at *Branch Office's* burned-out remains. Thick, acrid smoke drifted upward, into the darkness, covering the marina in the unsettling aroma of charred plastic, wood, and metal.

The San Juan County Fire and Rescue team had reacted quickly and though they were unable to save the yacht, they had managed to contain the fire to ensure no other vessels had been damaged. While grateful for that, Roland remained both troubled and traumatized over the yacht's sudden destruction. Adele, trying to stay dry under her umbrella, sensed his grief and rage. *This likely wasn't an accident, and he has a very good idea who was responsible.*

"You gonna be okay?" she asked.

Roland turned around with his hands stuffed into the pockets of his winter jacket, his face covered in a layer of wet soot. He exhaled loudly through his nose, shrugged, and then through clenched teeth, said, "It was Yuri. It *had* to be him. Sergei would never do something like this unless the order came from Yuri himself. That son of a bitch never wanted to buy *Branch Office*. He just came here to confirm what she was worth. He intended to burn it down all along."

"You should tell Lucas about that."

Roland's head lowered as he considered the well-intended advice. Adele watched and waited as he ran a hand through his wet hair and then growled his disagreement. "No. You don't go to the police when you're dealing with people like Yuri Popov."

"It wasn't that long ago you were telling me these people were just business associates."

Roland looked up at Adele. She saw something dangerously volatile in his eyes, a smoldering discontent that threatened potential violence. When he replied, it was in a voice Adele no longer recognized. In the span of a few minutes, Roland Soros had become a stranger to her. "I know how to handle my business. Make no mistake, what happened here *was* business."

Another familiar voice joined the conversation, causing Roland to go quiet and look away. "What business?"

Adele was grateful for Lucas's arrival, thinking Roland needed to be talked down from whatever plans for revenge against the Russians he might be unwisely contemplating.

Lucas, dressed in a dark, hooded rain jacket with the words "Sheriff's Department" emblazoned in big yellow letters on the back, ignored Roland's sulking silence and proceeded to update him on the investigation into the fire. "I interviewed the few people who were still around here when the fire started. Nobody indicated anything unusual. I assume the vessel is fully insured?"

Roland's lips drew back as he delivered a snarling rebuke. "What the hell does *that* have to do with anything?"

"I was just stating what I figured was likely, Roland. Now I'm wondering why you're so defensive. Anything you need to get off your chest?"

Roland stepped forward. "All I need from *you*, Lucas, is to mind your own damn business and stay out of mine."

Adele looked down and saw Roland's tightly clenched fists. Lucas, standing beside her, noticed them as well.

"Are you going to try to hit me, Roland? If you are, I suggest you reconsider. I hit back."

Roland looked down at his feet, shut his eyes, and sighed. "Just let me know if you find out anything regarding the fire, Sheriff."

Adele and Lucas watched as Roland moved past them. He walked quickly toward the main dock and then stopped and turned around, looking at Adele. "I would still like to talk with you about what happened."

Roland half turned to continue leaving but paused once again, this time to speak to Lucas. "I am sorry about your dad. I know what it's like to lose your family and feel all alone."

After Roland resumed his departure and disappeared fully into the night's gloom, Adele sensed Lucas's gaze falling upon her from above. "What does he need to speak to you about?" he asked.

With panic tightening her throat, Adele struggled to appear as if Roland's request was of little importance. Though what she disclosed wasn't quite an outright lie, it also managed to fall far short of the entire truth. "Oh, it's nothing. Just a personal matter." She watched Lucas bite down on his lower lip. *He doesn't believe me.*

"Uh-huh." Lucas's response was followed by an uncomfortable silence that said far more. Adele knew he suspected she was hiding something from him.

"My office received the toxicology report back on Carl Blime. It was definitely an overdose. We also had another death this morning, a teenage girl on Orcas."

Adele nodded, grateful Lucas had decided to change the subject. "Yes, Bess told me about it. Do you think it was drug-related?"

"Yeah, I do. I still have to interview the parents tomorrow. There will be another toxicology report to wait on, but from what Chancee already included in her initial report, drugs appear likely. The parents indicated their daughter's behavior had been noticeably different lately—more erratic."

Adele knew Lucas was referring to twenty-five-year-old Chancee Smith, one of two deputy sheriffs who worked under Lucas and oversaw the Orcas Island substation. The other deputy was Gunther Fox, a retired military veteran who worked on nearby Lopez Island.

Lucas ran a hand down his face, his tone reflecting equal parts frustration and dejection. "I've got to find out how these drugs are coming in, Adele, and who's responsible. That girl was just fifteen years old, a stupid kid wrapped up in all the nonsense that comes with being that young and thinking you're so much older than you really are."

"Lucas, you look tired. You should be home getting some rest."

"Home? Not with Dad gone. That was his home. My mother's home. *Our* home. I don't know if it can be my home anymore."

A gust of wind threatened to pull the umbrella out of Adele's hands. "It'll just take some time. You need to process your father's passing."

Lucas stared at what little remained of Roland's yacht. "What I need is to do my job. That's all that matters right now. Seemingly healthy people are dying and I need to figure out how to stop it from happening again." He reached out and gave Adele a quick hug. "Hey, I appreciate your support. You're right. It's just going to take me some time. My dad's service is next week—Thursday. Will you be able to make it?"

Adele hugged Lucas back. "Of course I'll be there. Now do like I said and try to get some rest."

Soon after, Adele stood on the dock alone, still fighting to keep the wind from ripping the umbrella from her grasp. She made the short walk back to her sailboat, feeling the effects of the long day and all the emotional turmoil that accompanied it. *I need to take my own advice and get some rest, too.*

After stepping onto the boat, Adele prepared to make her way inside but stopped to peer at something pinned to the companionway door. *What the hell is that?*

With the tips of her fingers, she pulled out a tack holding a small, square piece of paper in place. It was a matchbook. She opened it and found it nearly full, missing just a single match.

"A shame what happened to Mr. Soros's boat. She was a real beauty. Been a fixture of this marina for as long as I can recall."

Adele let out a startled yelp, almost dropping the matchbook. She turned around to see a tall, very thin middle-aged man smiling back at her. He also held onto an umbrella. His thin yellowish hair, when combined with his sunken face, reminded Adele of an emaciated scarecrow. A slash of a mustache resided over a narrow, almost nonexistent upper lip.

"I am so sorry. I didn't mean to startle you. My name is Bryce Workman. I'm the county park ranger. And you, well, I already *know* you. You're the young woman who writes all those wonderful stories for the newspaper. I heard you had settled into Delroy's old boat. It's nice to finally meet you. I just wish it was under better circumstances."

Adele dropped the matchbook into her pocket and then reached out across the sailboat's railing to shake the park ranger's extended hand, which she noted had a rough, sandpaper quality to it. "It's nice to meet you, too, Mr. Workman. I'm Adele—Adele Plank."

"I was just passing by Ms. Plank. I'll let you get inside. I'm heading home myself."

Bryce paused to look up at the sailboat's tall mast that loomed directly over Adele's head. "Was a lucky thing that Mr. Soros's vessel was at the end of the dock and not in a slip surrounded by a bunch of other boats. I've seen the results of a fire that started on a boat like yours and then jumps from one slip to the other, taking a whole mess of boats with it. Now that's the kind of tragedy that gets people killed. Yes, sir, this marina was fortunate tonight's fire was so well contained. It could have been much worse."

He gave Adele another smile. "Well, you take care now, Ms. Plank. I'm looking forward to the next issue of the paper."

Before he could turn to leave, Adele made certain to raise her voice loud enough that she was easily heard over the wind. "You can call me Adele."

Bryce stopped, appearing slightly confused. "What?"

"I said you can just call me Adele. And that means I can address you as Bryce, right? Unless you have a problem with that or wish to keep it more formal."

Bryce stammered, caught off guard by Adele's sudden focus on their respective names. "Uh, yeah, that's fine. Call me Bryce. All my friends do. What few I have, anyway."

Adele lowered her umbrella, allowing the rain to land on her directly. She smiled and nodded at the increasingly uncomfortable park ranger. "Weren't you the one who contacted Sheriff Pine late yesterday regarding a suspicious boat docked out at Matia Island?"

Bryce looked up at Adele from underneath heavy-lidded eyes. "Yeah, that was me. Lucas asked that I keep an eye out for him."

Adele's smile remained on her face as she trapped Bryce's gaze within hers. "I know. He told me. We went out there together to take a look but didn't find anything."

"Guess the boat took off before you got there. It wasn't exactly boating weather."

Adele wiped the rain from her eyes while still keeping her smile intact. "Yeah, had quite a bit of snow last night, but *you* were out on the water despite the bad weather. I mean, that's how you saw the boat tied up to the dock at Matia, right?"

Bryce's eyes darted from side to side as he scowled. "Are you interrogating me, Ms. Plank?"

"We just agreed that you could call me Adele, remember? And as far as my questions, I'm just trying to line up the facts for the newspaper."

Bryce shook his head. "I don't want to be part of any newspaper story. I was just helping the sheriff out."

"No worries. I'll refer to you as an anonymous source, okay? So just to be clear, you saw that boat yesterday, the one with the *dark-blue* hull. The one you spoke to Lucas about. It was tied up to the dock at Matia?"

Bryce's agitation was evident as he glared at Adele. "Yes. Now, if you don't mind, I'd like to get out of this rain and get home."

Adele extended her hand toward the marina entrance. "Yes, of course. And thank you for speaking with me. If I have any further questions, can I contact you? I'm sure I can get your number from Sheriff Pine."

Bryce turned and began to make his way down the dock, muttering as he did so. "Yeah, whatever."

Adele watched him go while contemplating what his motivation was for having just lied to her.

13

The Island Gazette
Islander Found Dead on Matia Island.

Carl Blime, aged forty-seven, was discovered lying unresponsive in his fishing boat by a local kayaker during early-morning hours last week. Mr. Blime's vessel was found floating against the Matia Island public dock. Blime was a longtime resident of the islands, noted for his love of fishing and the outdoors.

San Juan County Sheriff Lucas Pine subsequently indicated a just-concluded toxicology report suggests drugs were likely to have contributed to Mr. Blime's death. The sheriff's office requests that island residents be on the lookout for illegally imported prescription drugs. These drugs are said to lack the strict quality controls required for the legal distribution and sale of prescribed drugs, making the risk of overdose much higher. It is believed these drugs may be circulating on the islands now and are being made available to residents, both young and old. Anyone with information regarding this matter is asked to contact the sheriff's office directly.

Avery gave an approving nod as he finished reading the lead story for the next issue of the paper. "That will do just fine, Adele. I particularly like the photographs you took of Matia. It provides a fascinating contrast between the beauty of that area and the troubling information that accompanies the story of Mr. Blime's death. Tell me, how concerned should we be regarding those rogue pills the sheriff mentioned?"

Bess stood next to her husband. The old couple eagerly awaited Adele's response.

"I would say very concerned. At this point, Lucas doesn't know how many of those pills are floating around here or where they are coming from. And now with the death of that girl on Orcas, it seems we might be facing an epidemic."

Bess clicked her tongue against the roof of her mouth while shaking her head. "What's become of this world? How can people put things into their bodies when they don't really even know what it is? Why is everyone so determined to numb their pain? Life is painful sometimes. You just deal with it."

Bess continued to shake her head as she shuffled off toward the front of the office, leaving Adele and Avery alone in the back room. Avery sat down at the computer to complete the layout process. His right hand began to tremble as he attempted to move the mouse pad and begin his work. He quickly covered the hand with the other and pulled them toward his narrow chest.

"Dammit! Seems every day the shaking gets worse."

Adele had become accustomed to Avery's trembling but noticed it appeared to have worsened in recent weeks. "Can I get you anything? Are you cold? I can turn the heat up."

The longtime newspaperman grunted. "No, it'll pass. I'm fine. It just takes longer to get all this done. Bess keeps telling me to let Jose do more of the work. He's a whiz with this stuff. I suppose it's time I admit she's right."

Avery looked up at Adele from his seat in front of the computer. "Say, what do you think about us making Jose a partner in the business, too? It wouldn't come out of your share. Bess and I, we could make it so us three were minority partners and you were the majority partner. And then when we finally step away from the business for good, you and Jose will take the remaining shares, meaning you'll still be in charge but he'll have a reason to stay and continue helping you out."

Jose had already been overseeing distribution for the *Island Gazette* and more recently maintaining the paper's online presence, which had greatly increased the publication's profits. Adele knew him to be a devoted worker who likely would have stayed on with the paper regardless of being given an ownership stake. But she was happy to see his efforts and talents deservedly rewarded. "I'm fine with whatever you and Bess decide, Avery, so long as you promise me you're not thinking of retiring just yet."

Avery rubbed the top button of his heavy cardigan sweater between his bone-thin fingers. "Well, as I said to you before, I'm not getting any younger. I'm about the same age as Dr. Pine was, you know. Speaking of which, how is Lucas doing?"

"Actually, I'm heading over there as soon as I leave here to check in on him. He's hurting, but he's a strong man and his job helps to keep his mind occupied."

Avery scrolled through several photos Adele had taken of Roland's yacht as it had burned. They intended to make the fire a last-minute addition to the upcoming edition. "And what of Mr. Soros? It seems both those young men are dealing with difficult times."

Adele's answer to Avery's question about Roland was far less immediate, something she knew to be a reflection of the conflicted nature that was her current relationship with the wealthy businessman. "Roland is understandably upset, but losing a boat isn't the same as losing a father. He'll be fine."

Avery leaned back in his chair and stuck out his lower lip, giving him the appearance of a particularly contemplative, elderly bulldog. "Hmmm, you might be right about Mr. Soros, but then again, a person born into wealth and then left alone with only that wealth to keep him company might be just as stricken by grief at the loss of something so grand, so representative of great privilege as that yacht was to him. Those with money are often the ones most uncomfortable over the prospect of losing it."

Adele's brows drew together. She worried Avery might be right about Roland's misplaced priorities.

"Ah, I'm just an old man rambling," Avery said. "Mr. Soros has been a wonderful supporter of our little paper. My words were bad manners, nothing more. I should know better."

"You said nothing wrong. Roland is a complicated subject for me right now."

Avery's eyes widened. He began to open his mouth to inquire as to what Adele meant by complication, then remembered his own recent admission of it being rude to speak of someone who wasn't there.

Adele reached down to give his narrow shoulders a light squeeze. "Don't work too hard. I'm off to visit with the sheriff."

Avery's still-trembling hand gave the top of Adele's hand a warm pat. "Tell him hello for us. I'll be working on his father's obituary later today."

Adele promised she would let Lucas know, waved goodbye to Bess who stood behind the counter in the front of the office, and then made her way outside and to her MINI parked on a side street half a block away. The air was unusually warm, the first true hint of the coming spring that still remained several weeks away. The Friday Harbor streets were nearly empty, with several storefronts closed and dark, awaiting the return of the summer tourists.

Right before getting into her car, Adele spotted Roland walking out of the Friday Harbor Insurance building. He appeared deep in thought, his face marked by a pronounced scowl. She thought to yell hello, then lowered her arm, deciding against it as she recalled how defensive Roland was following Lucas's question to him regarding the insurance on *Branch Office*.

A policy for something like that could easily be hundreds of thousands of dollars, possibly more.

Even for a man of Roland Soros's means, that was real money, especially if his funds were tied up in the Cattle Point project as he had already indicated they were. Adele watched him slide behind the wheel of his black Mercedes and then drive off. He remained oblivious to her presence no more than fifty yards away, despite his request just last night that he wished to speak with her.

Adele recalled how angry Roland was following the fire that destroyed his yacht. It was a change so drastic, so out of character with the man she knew, it felt as if he had momentarily become a stranger to her. *Maybe the man I saw last night was the real Roland Soros—angry, reckless, and possibly vengeful. Avery might have been on to something. I might have no idea how far Roland would go to keep what's his no matter how dangerous the people he thinks are trying to take it from him are.*

A quick check of her phone told Adele it was nearly noon. The sheriff's office receptionist, Samantha Boyler, had already informed Adele that Lucas had been scheduled to return back from his Orcas Island interview on the 11:00 a.m. interisland ferry.

Just as Adele went to place her phone into her coat pocket, it rang. She looked down and was surprised to see it was a call from Samantha. The receptionist's tone betrayed the concern that had motivated her to make the call to Adele.

"Hello, Ms. Plank. I'm sorry to bother you, but I was wondering if you had seen or heard from Sheriff Pine yet?"

"No. Is he still on Orcas Island conducting the interview?"

"Well, that's just it," Samantha said. "The sheriff never showed up at the parents' home. I already checked with ferry personnel, and they have no record of him getting on the morning ferry." As she further explained the details of the sheriff's unusual absence, Samantha's tone grew more desperate. Where Adele was somewhat concerned, Samantha was already near panic. "This isn't like the sheriff at all, Ms. Plank. I've tried to reach him by phone, but he won't pick up. He *always* responds to my calls."

"I'm on my way to his home right now, Samantha. I'm sure everything is fine. I'll let you know what I find out."

"Thank you, Ms. Plank. Call me as soon as you know something."

Adele took a deep breath, pushing away her own panic while she looked down both ends of the empty street. As she started her car and put it into gear, her mind repeated a mantra she hoped would prove true. *Lucas is okay. Lucas is okay.*

The drive to reach the Pine residence took just a few minutes but felt much longer. Lucas's SUV was parked in front of the home. Adele pulled in behind it, turned off her car, and stepped outside. She was struck by how still the air was. Normally, even on the calmest of days, a slight breeze pushed its way through the area. Adele looked up the paved walkway to the covered porch and saw the window curtains had been pulled shut.

Lucas is okay. Lucas is okay.

Each step to the front door seemed unusually loud as Adele's shoes scuffed against the concrete path and the chipped-paint steps. Her hand hesitated, hovering in front of the doorbell before finally pushing it. Hearing no movement from inside, Adele pushed it again, and then again.

The home remained unnaturally still.

Like a tomb.

Adele cursed herself for giving life to such a horrible thought. She moved to one of the large front windows and pressed her face to the glass, trying to look inside. She saw the outline of furniture, but the rooms were dark. She felt her heart beating inside her chest as she rapped on the glass.

"Lucas, are you home? It's Adele."

Again, no answer.

Try the backdoor.

Adele scurried to the back yard, reaching the kitchen door in seconds. She turned the handle, silently praying for it to be unlocked.

It was.

She opened the door and stepped into the kitchen, finding it as dark as the rooms at the front of the home. Unwashed dishes filled the sink. Two empty beer bottles sat on the counter.

"Lucas!"

Adele moved through the first floor of the home and found each room empty. She paused at the bottom of the stairs, looking into the darkness that greeted her from the second floor hallway.

Lucas is okay. Lucas is okay.

Every time Adele spoke those words in her mind, the tightening in her stomach became worse as her subconscious whispered of something terrible awaiting her upstairs. She didn't want to see it but knew she must.

A creak sounded from the bottom step, followed by another and yet another as Adele took the steps two at a time. She reached the hallway and saw light coming from a partially open door to her left.

The bathroom.

"Lucas, are you up here?"

Adele strained to detect any response, any noise, any sign of life. She thought she heard a stirring of something coming from the bathroom. *Only one way to find out.*

She walked slowly down the hallway to the bathroom door, knocked, and waited, sensing the presence of someone or something on the other side. She took a deep breath.

Lucas is okay. Lucas is okay.

The door hinges screeched loudly as Adele pushed it open.

Inside, she found Lucas Pine.

He wasn't okay.

14

Unable to stir him, Adele proceeded to slap Lucas in the face—hard.

The sound echoed off the bathroom walls.

One of his eyes was partially open while the other remained closed.

"Lucas—WAKE UP!"

Lucas groaned. His legs straightened, causing some of the water in the tub to splash out onto the linoleum floor. His voice was a dry croak, accompanied by breath so sour, Adele had to turn her face away.

"Hey, what are you doing here?"

An empty bottle of whiskey floated in the tub directly above Lucas's midsection. Sitting atop the closed toilet seat next to the tub was a box overflowing with photographs of his mother and father. His eyes finally opened fully. He looked around, clearly confused over why he was shivering in a bathtub full of cold water.

"What the hell?"

Adele turned away again. This time it wasn't Lucas's breath but rather that the empty whiskey bottle had drifted to the end of the tub, leaving the sheriff's midsection fully exposed just beneath the tub water's clear surface.

"If I were to take a guess, I'd say you got very drunk last night and passed out in the bathtub. You're lucky you didn't drown or suffer hypothermia. Samantha is worried sick. You missed your interview with the parents of the girl who died on Orcas."

Lucas covered his face with his hands. He remained like that for nearly a minute before the hands moved away from his face and clung to the sides of the tub. "I need to stand."

Adele stood up and backed away. "Then do it. I'll go downstairs and make some coffee."

Lucas closed his eyes again and grimaced. "Wait, I think I need your help." He held up his hand, wanting Adele to assist him in getting up. Her eyes darted to the towel rack and found it empty.

"Uh, you're not wearing any clothes."

Lucas glanced down at his naked body and then looked up at Adele. "Modesty isn't really a high priority for me right now. I just need to dry off before I'm permanently wrinkled. C'mon, I need you to pull."

Adele took Lucas's hand, shut her eyes tight, and pulled. He rose up with a loud splash as water dripped down his tall, muscular form. He stood on unsteady legs, momentarily swaying from side to side. Adele was certain if she let go, he would topple over.

"Uh-oh."

Adele opened her eyes and noticed the color had completely drained from his face. "Uh-oh, *what*?"

Lucas turned around, placed his hands on the wall and hung his head between his arms, giving Adele a full view of his backside. "I'm gonna be sick. You might want to close the door."

Adele was quick to comply, wanting nothing to do with being witness to someone vomiting in the nude. She moved into the hallway and closed the door behind her. "I'll go downstairs and make some coffee. You come down when you're ready."

The reply was a guttural retching noise as Lucas made good on his promise of feeling sick. He let Adele know he heard her with a weak "okay" and then he resumed throwing up.

Adele made her way downstairs and into the kitchen. Soon the coffee machine was gurgling away while she prepared scrambled eggs, one of her personal favorite hangover meals. By the time the coffee was done and the eggs were plated, she heard footsteps coming down the stairs. Lucas emerged wearing a tattered bathrobe and slippers. His eyes appeared to be having trouble focusing, and his slow shuffle indicated he was still debilitated by the amount of alcohol consumed the night before. He made his way to the sink, filled a glass with water, drank it down, and then took a few unsteady steps to his left and opened a cupboard, from which he took out a bottle of Pepto-Bismol and another bottle of aspirin. Five aspirin were emptied into his hand. Lucas washed the aspirin down with three loud gulps of the pink liquid Pepto.

He tried to give Adele a smile, but one side of his mouth was unwilling to complete the task, leaving the sad effort with nothing more to show for it than a badly lopsided grin. "I'm already on the road to recovery. Thanks for waking me up and helping me out of the damn tub."

Adele watched Lucas shuffle toward the kitchen table and then stop and turn around. He appeared to suddenly have remembered something that bothered him. "Just to be clear, that water was *really* cold."

Adele placed a plate of scrambled eggs and a cup of coffee on the kitchen table and motioned for Lucas to sit down with her. She was relieved to hear him attempting to make a joke of what had happened, thinking it meant he was in the initial stages of coming to terms with his father's death. After taking a sip of coffee, she shrugged.

"I don't know if I'd necessarily call the water cold as much as *cool*, Sheriff. And certainly not cold enough to cause any kind of undo shrinkage." Adele made the statement so matter of fact it caused Lucas to pause with his coffee cup halfway between table and mouth. He stared at Adele, waiting for her to crack a smile and give up the joke. She ignored his eyes in favor of keeping the good-natured torture going.

"I can remember being told when I was a girl fishing in a pond how the water made the fish look bigger than they really were. I never gave it much thought, but then you see something years later and realize sometimes those things you were told as a kid really are true!"

Lucas put his coffee down and pointed across the table at Adele. "Now hold on, you're having way too much fun kicking a guy when he's in a bad way."

Adele put her cup down and pretended to give long and serious consideration to what Lucas said, until finally, she nodded. "I believe you're right, Sheriff. I don't know what's come over me. For some reason, I'm being rather *small*."

"Ha-ha. Are you done?" Lucas folded his arms over his chest. "Can we change the subject? Or do you want to keep making shrinkage jokes? I'm telling you, that water was freezing."

Both Adele and Lucas proceeded to finish what remained of their coffee in silence. With the temporary respite of teasing concluded, the reality of Dr. Pine's passing returned. Lucas's hands rested on the table with the coffee cup between them. His face lifted, revealing eyes that had seen far too little rest.

"What happened last night?" Adele asked.

Lucas chewed slowly, cocked his head, and sighed. "I came home and decided to try and go to bed early. I lay there for a few hours but couldn't get to sleep. So, I got up, opened a beer, went into my dad's study, and came out with that box of pictures you found. Started looking through them, had another beer, and then, I don't know, things just kind of fell apart for me inside this house. I just felt so alone. It was unbearably empty in here but suffocating at the same time, like the air had gone stale. I told you it was going to be tough for me to come back here. That's when I got into the whiskey and kept looking at photographs. I remember deciding to run a bath but don't recall much after that. Next thing I know, you're smacking me across the face, and I'm puking my guts out."

Adele watched him have another bite of egg. He cleared his throat while rubbing the remaining sleep out of his eyes. "I messed up. There's no excuse. Getting piss-drunk is the last thing Dad would have wanted me to do. I want to apologize to you for your having to see me like this. I'll give a similar apology to Samantha. I called her when I was upstairs to let her know I'd be coming into the office soon."

"You're going to work?"

Lucas appeared surprised at the question. "Yeah. I don't work a typical nine to five any more than you do. Things need to be done that can't wait. The last ferry to Orcas leaves in an hour. I intend to be on it. Those parents deserve to know I'm doing all I can to find out the circumstances of their daughter's death. Besides, I'm already feeling much better thanks to you."

He got up from the table. "Thank you again for the coffee, the food—for everything. You're welcome to stick around here if you want."

Adele stood as well, sensing Lucas wanted to hurry up, get dressed, and be on his way. She had intended to speak with him about questions she had concerning the park ranger, Bryce Workman, but decided his proverbial plate was already full at the moment. That conversation would have to wait, most likely until after his father's service later that week.

"No. I'll get going. If you need anything just give me a call."

Lucas wrapped his arms around Adele and gave her a long hug. He didn't seem to want to let go but eventually stepped back and tilted his head toward the stairs. "Well, I suppose I should be getting cleaned up. If I hear anything newsworthy while I'm on Orcas, I'll let you know."

When she opened the front door and stepped out onto the covered porch, Adele was greeted by the sight and sound of rainfall. She took out her phone to check the time and found an unread text message from Roland. He asked that she stop by his home as soon as possible.

The message was marked urgent.

15

It would be the first time Adele had been invited to see the inside of Roland's home. She knew the location. It was a narrow, paved, and gated drive to a large property on a hill overlooking the entirety of the Friday Harbor marina. She had texted him back confirming she was on her way and then he replied with the three-digit gate code: 1-8-1.

The nine-foot-high black iron gate blocking the driveway had the name SOROS prominently displayed in bold, gold lettering at the top. A shorter fence similar in style was attached to both sides of the gate and appeared to enclose the entirety of the vast property.

Adele waited for the gate to slide open and then drove her MINI down the drive toward what was a surprisingly modest, single-story rambler painted brown with gray trim. The home's simplicity was further exemplified by the surrounding grass and shrubbery. Though tasteful and well-manicured, the landscaping did not live up to the show of wealth the gated entrance promised.

A circular drive marked the front of the small home. Adele parked directly behind Roland's black Mercedes, stepped out of her car, and was immediately greeted by a tall, red-bearded man dressed in a heavy black winter jacket and matching black slacks. He appeared to be in his late twenties, heavily built with a significant belly, and he had light-blue eyes that looked out from beneath a set of especially bushy red eyebrows.

It wasn't until he walked around the hood of her car that Adele noticed the man was carrying a hunting rifle. He saw her eyes widen with alarm and immediately attempted to ease her fears "Ms. Plank, my name is Justin Allen. I'm an old classmate of Roland's. He recently hired me to help out with security at his home. Right this way please."

Before Justin could turn to begin the walk toward the home, the front door opened, and Roland emerged holding a handgun. Adele watched his eyes dart toward the end of the driveway, making certain Adele had not been followed. His normally immaculate appearance was now the opposite: unwashed hair, rumpled clothes, and an agitated, near-manic aura that alarmed Adele to the point that she considered getting back into her car and driving away.

Roland motioned for her to follow him inside. "I apologize for the weapons. These are troubled times, and I'm merely a man forced to take precautions." He turned around. "This is Justin. We went to school together. He actually played football on the varsity team with Lucas. I needed someone to keep an eye out for me while I'm here."

Roland's words crashed together with stream-of-consciousness-like speed. His face was covered in an oily layer of sweat, an appearance made worse by a noticeable tick in the corner of his left eye. "C'mon, c'mon, let's get inside. We need to talk."

Adele paused at the home's entrance, sensing her initial concern for Roland was transforming into fear *of* him. "I'll come in, but only if you put that gun away."

Roland looked down seemingly unaware he was holding a firearm. "Sure, come on in. I'll put this thing away. Close the door behind you and lock it, please."

The home's interior was dark and smelled of stale cigarettes. The lime-green wallpaper and burnt-red shag carpet was a retro time machine, marking the home as having not been updated since the 1970s. A short hallway opened up into the main living area, dominated by pastels and teak furnishings that were also decades old. What wasn't dated but instead was timeless were the incredible views afforded by the floor-to-ceiling windows overlooking Friday Harbor. From Roland's living room, Adele could see the town's seaside streets, the ferry terminal, the marina, and the waters beyond.

"Yeah, that's the money-shot right there," Roland said. "In the summer, when it's clear you can see all the way out to Mount Baker from here. Hey, uh, can I get you something to drink? Water, juice, whatever you want."

Adele pulled her gaze away from the view to address Roland directly. "I'm fine, but you're still holding the gun."

Roland put the gun down onto the teak-framed glass coffee table in the middle of the living room that was also home to an almost-full ashtray and several empty cans of energy drink. He motioned for Adele to take a seat on the couch opposite the matching reclining chair he fell into. He folded and unfolded his hands several times on his lap, all the while avoiding looking directly at Adele.

"What the hell is going on, Roland? The guy outside with the rifle? You locked up in here with a weapon? This isn't you."

Roland's head bobbed up and down. "I know. It's getting pretty crazy, all this stuff with Sergei and Yuri, the boat fire, the Cattle Point project. It's all a big mess right now. It'll be fine, though. It'll be fine. I'll handle it."

Adele scowled. "What I'm seeing right now isn't someone 'handling it.' You look like you're having a nervous breakdown."

Roland wiped his forehead with the back of his hand. "No, I'm fine, really. I'm just, you know, working things out in my head. These Russians? Yeah, it's gotten a little scary. And that has me plenty pissed off. It will be dealt with. One way or the other, I'll take care of it."

"Are you sure it was the Russians who started the fire?"

Roland grunted. "Yeah, I'm sure. No doubt about it."

Adele leaned forward on the couch, trying to get a better look at Roland's eyes. "Why would they want to destroy your boat? I thought you were selling it to Yuri?"

Roland wagged a finger and shook his head. "No, no, that's what I thought, too. Yuri just wanted to confirm the boat was there and see how much it was worth. He intended to burn it down all along. You see, either he gets me to hand over to him the insurance payment or he puts me so far behind in what I owe him that I have no choice but to sign over the entire Cattle Point project to him. After I've done all the real work, the property acquisitions, the environmental impact studies, campaign donations to county and state politicians, the permits, the designs, nearly four million dollars of my own money sitting out there long before the first parking lot will be paved, let alone the first dollar made back. Almost every cent of all my liquid assets has been put into Cattle Point. Yuri figured that out, and now he's trying to break me so he can take it over for pennies on the dollar. God help us all if a man like Yuri Popov were to succeed in doing that. He'll bleed these islands dry before he's finished."

Adele felt little sympathy for Roland but plenty of anger. "Then why in the hell did you allow someone like Yuri to be a partner in your business, Roland? Were you so arrogant to believe you could control a man like that? Look at where it's got you! Sitting inside your home with a gun, worried over who might be knocking on your door next. Have you told Lucas about Yuri? He's the sheriff. He can help you."

Roland looked as if he had smelled something offensive. "No, he can't. Lucas Pine can barely help himself. He does have something to do with my asking you to be here, though."

Adele's brows lifted as she waited for Roland to continue. "C'mon, Adele, you're a smart woman. It's no secret Lucas has feelings for you, and obviously you and I have feelings for each other, given what took place between us the other day."

Adele started to say something but was cut off by Roland, who held up his hand. "Wait, let me finish. I need you to know I have no regrets about what happened. I just hope that you feel the same. So do you?"

Given Roland's stress levels and fragile emotional condition, Adele knew she should proceed with caution. "Roland, I'm not sure this is the best time for this particular conversation. You clearly have more important things to deal with right now."

Outside, a ferry's horn wailed, signaling its departure from Friday Harbor. Roland looked out the window, wiped the bottom of his nose with the back of his hand, and then shook his head. "Please don't try and tell me what the right time to feel something is, Adele. If you're unwilling to answer that simple question how about an even simpler one?"

"What question is that?"

Roland's jaw clenched as he loudly expelled air from his flared nostrils. "Why?"

Adele frowned. "What do you mean?"

Roland licked his lips, appearing to battle against some unseen war raging within him. "Why did you sleep with me? I know why I slept with you. It's because I care about you. I'm attracted to you. I want to be close to you."

Adele stammered, unprepared to give a response that might satisfy Roland and his hopes for a relationship beyond their one-time sexual encounter. "I don't know, Roland. It just happened. We were together. It was a moment we shared. And like you, I don't regret it, even if I don't entirely understand why it happened. It just did. I'll also repeat what I said before—that shouldn't be your priority right now. You have some very serious issues going on with your business. Issues you just admitted could negatively impact the entire community. Have you even considered the possibility the same Russians you've been partnering with on Cattle Point could also be engaged in illegal activity on the islands? That perhaps Yuri Popov's interest in your Cattle Point complex is to use it as a distribution center for drugs, prostitution, illegal gambling, and whatever else a man like that is involved in?"

Roland looked away. It was a gesture Adele took as proof he had in fact thought over that very thing. He wrapped his arms around himself, as if he were suddenly cold. "Why would you ask that? Do you know something?"

Adele waited for Roland to look at her before she continued. "I know last summer we had a young woman, a Russian who came here from Vancouver, murdered. Now while Lucas helped me to prove that murder didn't directly involve the Vancouver Russians you've been dealing with, the fact remains she was here on the island working at a restaurant in a building *you* own. We also know she wasn't an American citizen and was working there illegally."

Roland's eyes flared as he held up both hands, palms out, in front of him. "I appreciate all the thought you've given this, but I just own the building, not the business. I have nothing to do with the hiring decisions. I'm just the landlord."

"Correct," Adele said. "And I would guess that before Yuri gave you money to keep your Cattle Point project going, you had to inform him of those property assets, including what kind of businesses they were, right?"

Roland shrugged. "I'm not following what this has to do with Cattle Point."

"Well, what if Yuri's been sending workers to those businesses to engage in illegal activity? Maybe he was testing things out, getting a feel for the level of local law enforcement he might have to deal with after he took over Cattle Point."

Roland's chin fell to his chest as he contemplated the possibilities being outlined by Adele. "Making me the door Yuri uses to walk through. A man like him would be earning money off every angle. Payment to secure the jobs here for the illegal workers he transports from Vancouver, likely an ongoing percentage of their wages, drug sales, prostitution, yeah, I'll concede that's all *possible*. I don't know how likely, but . . ."

Adele easily accepted Roland's residual uncertainty because she also shared at least some of it with him. "I know it sounds crazy, but if you're already convinced Yuri Popov was willing to destroy your yacht it seems prudent at this point to consider the worst where he's concerned. Are you going to give him the money you received from the insurance policy on *Branch Office*?"

"If I do that, how long before he sets fire to something else? Maybe one of the buildings I own. I would just be rewarding him for pushing me around, making it even more likely he does it again. The fire was a test to see if I gave up. Besides, my insurance won't be so quick to pay out on another fire. There would be a full investigation. Yuri has to know this. He doesn't care about the payment on the loan. He wants the whole thing. He wants Cattle Point. If he gets that, he'll take it all over. And everything these islands are to those of us who call this place home—there'll be nothing left."

"Then we stop that from happening—all of us, including Lucas. He has to be a part of this, Roland. Whatever competition you have with him, it needs to be put aside. And what happened between us, that needs to be put aside as well, at least for now. Give me your word you can do that. If not, I'm done here, and I'm done with you."

Roland straightened in his chair as his eyes lit up with a glimmer of his former, confident self. "Just like that?"

"Yeah, just like that."

Roland folded one leg over the other and chuckled. "Perhaps you should reconsider your profession. You're one hard-ass negotiator. I'm in. You, me, Lucas, whoever you think can help us keep Cattle Point out of the hands of Yuri. What's the plan?"

Adele was relieved to see more of the old Roland returning second by second. "I'm not exactly sure just yet. I want to give Lucas time to bury his father before bringing him up to speed. After the funeral we can all focus together on this Yuri Popov situation. Until then I need you to pull yourself together and I don't think that can happen with you hiding inside of this house. I'd like you to stay at the hotel in Roche Harbor. I can call ahead and have Tilda give you a room anonymously. You take a couple of days to rest, clean up, and clear your head. I'll drive. Leave your car here and don't tell anyone else where you're going."

Roland frowned. "What if Yuri sends someone here to burn my house down just like he did to *Branch Office*?"

Adele's eyes scanned the home's dated interior. Roland noticed her doing so and tapped the coffee table with a fingertip. "I know this place isn't much to look at, and this is going to sound weird, but I've kept it the same, *exactly* the same, as my grandparents had it. You know I don't smoke, just like I know you noticed the ashtray on the table there. Even that has been left as it was. I never emptied it after they were gone. Every day after he was done at the bank, my grandfather would sit in the same chair I'm sitting in now, smoking and looking out at all that water below us. I had planned to build my own place soon and keep this house just like it was, just like it is, for as long as I am around. Don't ask me to explain why, because I can't, at least not in a way that would make sense to someone else. I just don't want to change anything because it feels like as long as I keep it like this, they're still here with me. When I told Lucas I knew what it was like to be all alone, I meant it. Keeping this house the way it was when I was a kid, when my grandparents were still alive, helps me to feel as if I'm not so alone."

Whatever earlier anger Adele might have felt toward Roland dissipated. She knew then that if he was not an entirely broken man, Roland Soros was certainly a badly damaged one. "Have Justin stay here at the house. If he sees anything suspicious, have him call 9-1-1. Lucas can be out here within a few minutes. And in the meantime, you rest up in Roche Harbor and unplug from all this chaos. After Dr. Pine's service, we'll sit down and figure this out together."

Roland sunk farther into the chair, giving him the appearance of a tired child finally resigned to going to bed. "Okay I'll do it your way. Let me grab a few things. I'll let Justin know I'll be gone for a few days and then we can get going."

While Roland left to gather up a change of clothes Adele remained seated, her mind already forming a plan she felt required a return to Matia Island. This time, though, she would be going there alone.

16

Adele's early morning path to Matia was marked by glass-surface waters, blue skies, and a pod of cheerful, dark-skinned porpoises that followed alongside her for nearly a quarter mile before disappearing deeper below the surface on their way to whatever other destination awaited them in their world-beneath-the-world existence. The trip was another opportunity for Adele to take out Decklan Stone's classic fiberglass runabout the writer had left to her during his long absence from the islands. Her confidence and skill on the water had improved considerably since her first attempt to captain the small watercraft on her own last summer. Her ability to combine direction and throttle in both forward and reverse was now almost instinctive. Adele had come to learn and appreciate the boat's limitations, which she was certain far exceeded her own.

Due to the unusually calm winter waters, the runabout was able to skim across the sea surface at a rate of more than twenty knots without the harsh pounding that normally accompanied a small craft's progress at such speeds. The vessel's sharp bow cut through the saltwater with a satisfying hiss, while the outboard hanging off the stern left an impressively frothy, water-churning wake.

Within thirty minutes after leaving Roche Harbor, Adele spotted the multiple sandstone fingers of Sucia Island to her left and the smaller treed hump that was nearby Matia Island on the right. Unlike before, Adele had no intention of using Matia's public dock to gain access to the island. Instead, she steered the runabout toward the island's far less accessible southern shores, marked by steep rocks, swirling tide pools, and multiple beds of prop-tangling eel grass.

It took another twenty minutes of creeping slowly along the shoreline before Adele found a narrow opening between two partially submerged rocks and a fallen evergreen tree that was likely a casualty of the recent storm. Its lower half was still rooted in the soil of the island, but its upper trunk and branches lay over the water. Adele had to duck down below the runabout's windshield, but even then she felt a branch brush across the top of her head. Once past the fallen tree, she was rewarded with a tiny, ten-by-ten pebbly patch of beach she was able to point the bow into while tilting the outboard up to avoid damaging the engine's prop against the shallow sea bottom.

After having secured the runabout via a rope tied to nearby tree, Adele slung the backpack she'd brought with her over her shoulders and gazed up at the steep rock cliff that loomed directly in front of her. She looked to her right and then to her left, her eyes scanning for an opening in the thick, wet-green undergrowth.

That there might work.

Adele's "there" was a barely visible, hard-packed dirt path over a rock outcrop to her left that led upward into the island's southern hillside. She had spent an hour online the night before researching the history of Matia Island and had come to learn of the area's well-deserved, outlaw reputation as a former haven for water smugglers during the Prohibition era. Alcohol would travel down from Canada and be left in a multitude of island nooks and crannies where it would then find its way to mainland customers in Bellingham and beyond. Matia was among those islands most often used for such nefarious endeavors. And decades later, the remnants of trails used by those long-ago smugglers still crisscrossed the islands.

The going was difficult, leaving Adele gasping for breath as she scrabbled, pulled, and pushed her way up the narrow path while trying to avoid slipping on the crumbling dirt and pebble surface and plunging back down to the rock-strewn waters below. With each step, the backpack's weight grew heavier, creating a dull, pulling pain where the straps carved into the flesh of her shoulders. Her fingers repeatedly dug into the island soil, while the toes of her hiking boots did the same. Adele paused to rest and noted with a faint smile the dirt that had collected beneath her fingernails. She was reminded of something her since-departed grandmother on her father's side had said to her many years ago. Grandma Plank had been a hard woman, quick to anger. She had also been just as quick to defend and protect those she'd loved. She hadn't suffered fools easily and had had little patience for the superficialities of the modern world.

The two things she admired most in people were loyalty and hard work. Adele recalled the advice her grandmother gave her on the eve of Adele's thirteenth birthday:

"Soon enough you'll have to try and navigate the attention of boys, Adele. Don't pay much mind to the clothes they wear or the cars they drive. That's all phony pretend stuff meant to fool you. Look past the surface and find a man with an honest heart and a bit of dirt under his nails. That's someone who knows the value of something real, something earned; that's the kind of man you want by your side as you both set out, trying to deal with all the crap this life is certain to throw at you."

Adele turned around on the trail to look out upon the blue-green San Juan waters surrounding Matia Island and wondered what Grandma Plank would have thought of Roland Soros and Lucas Pine. Would she have believed either man worthy of Adele's time and consideration?

Not likely. She'd probably have run the both of them off with shotgun in hand.

Adele adjusted her backpack and resumed her slow, careful ascent toward the summit of the island's evergreen-and-pine-tree crown, a destination reached some twenty minutes later. Adele removed the backpack, unzipped the front of her winter jacket, and then leaned over with the palms of her hands resting against her blue-jean-clad knees. Droplets of sweat marked wet trails down the sides of her face as the muscles in her legs continued to protest the hard slog up the hillside. She focused on her breathing, taking long, deliberate gulps of air, until a short time later her fatigue subsided.

With her energy returned, Adele rose up, slung the backpack over her shoulders, and began to make her way toward the area overlooking the island's public dock where she had stood with Lucas on the morning he was informed by phone of his father's death. The place was as they had left it, with no evidence of anyone else having been there since. On this day, it would be where Adele intended to sit and wait.

Looking up, she was pleased to see only a few light clouds moving slowly overhead. The day would belong to the sun. Adele removed the backpack and sat next to it on the slightly moist, pine-needle-covered earth. She reached out to grab her toes, enjoying the feeling of her calf muscles being stretched, while also keeping an eye on the still, silent waters of Rolf Cove and the Matia boat dock below.

Minutes turned to hours as Adele remained waiting and watching until the inevitable shadows of late afternoon began to creep across the island. During that time, only two boats had passed by Matia, neither of which stopped at the dock. With the temperature dropping, Adele reached into the backpack and removed the portable propane heater she had brought with her. She set it down on the ground in front of her, opened the small tank's valve, pressed the igniter, and enjoyed the near-instant warmth the little device provided. From her place all the way at the top of the hill and hidden within the blanket of trees, Adele was confident she would remain hidden to anyone who might arrive at the dock below.

The heater served as a flameless campfire, keeping most of the approaching evening chill away. By the time the last of the daylight dissipated, Adele's stomach was growling. Again her hand went into the backpack, this time retrieving the peanut-butter-and-mayonnaise sandwich she had made prior to leaving Roche Harbor. That, too, was a combination given to her by Grandma Plank, which was comprised of two slices of white bread—peanut butter spread on one piece, mayonnaise slathered onto the other—followed by ample amounts of black pepper over the mayonnaise, after which both slices were brought together in a harmonious blend of creamy, sweet-and-savory goodness.

Adele was sitting in near darkness, happily finishing off the last of the sandwich, when her chewing slowed as she cocked her head at the familiar, deep-throated growl of an approaching vessel. Though she could not yet see the boat, the unmistakable high-horsepower tone of its dual engines informed Adele of its imminent arrival. She shut off the heater and then stood up with narrowed eyes straining to see through the gloom. A shadowy mass appeared at the entrance to Rolf Cove. The dark-blue cruiser was approaching the dock at a dangerously high rate of speed without the aid of any navigation lights.

It's a water version of stealth mode. Whoever is behind the wheel doesn't want to be seen. Judging by how confidently they're pulling up to the dock, they've done this many times before.

A wave created by the boat's high-speed approach slammed into the dock, causing the pilings to creak loudly. The boat soon followed, pulling up alongside the dock. Then, just as quickly, the engines were turned off and the island returned to its earlier silence. Adele considered using her phone to take photos of the boat and its driver but feared that without the flash, the pictures would only show darkness, while use of the flash would likely reveal her location.

She made her way as quietly as possible down the path toward the beach at the end of dock, hoping to confirm the presence of the man she was almost certain would be driving the boat. With her eyes already fully adjusted to the darkness and aided by a nearly full moon, Adele moved past the two small cedar buildings which housed the island's compost toilet facilities. She crouched behind a large shrub near where the dock joined with the beach and waited.

Soon, heavy footsteps echoed off the dock's wood planks, moving toward Adele with surprising speed. She feared having put herself too close to the dock, making her vulnerable to being seen. With eyes scanning the darkness for the next closest area of cover, Adele prepared to move, then froze, realizing it was already too late. She saw the shadowy outline of a broad-shouldered man nearing the shore. The moonlight reflected off his cleanly shaved head, revealing a lean, wolfish face, dark eyes, and a cruel slash of a mouth encased in a dark goatee.

Sergei Kozlov had arrived at Matia Island and now stood no more than a few paces from where Adele remained hiding, silent and wide-eyed, behind the shrub. She held her breath, praying Sergei would continue on his way to wherever it was on the island he intended to go. Though fearful, Adele took comfort in realizing that if need be, she was also ready to fight.

17

In his left hand, the Russian held a white plastic garbage sack. He paused at the trailhead to reach into a pocket with his other hand and withdrew a phone, which he promptly held up to his face. Initially he spoke in Russian but then switched to English.

"Yes, I make drop now. No, this time it was good—nobody here. Yuri, there are no worries. They are too busy chasing fires."

Sergei turned to his right and appeared to stare directly at Adele, who remained crouched and still, hoping the darkness would be enough to keep her from being discovered. "I do not know if he told them about the drop," he continued. "I only know there is nobody here now. If he is lying, I deal with it. Yuri, when have I ever failed you? This is all nothing. These people, they are frightened children. We do what we want on these islands. It is good. Nothing has changed. You are separated from all of this. You remain protected as always. Cattle Point will be yours. Yes, of course. Okay. I return to Vancouver soon."

Sergei slipped the phone back into the front pocket of his black wool jacket. His dark eyes remained fixed upon the shrub behind which Adele was hiding. He dropped the garbage sack, reached back into his jacket, withdrew a pack of cigarettes and a lighter, and proceeded to have a smoke. Each time he expelled a cloud of tobacco-laden air from his lungs, the Russian would mumble to himself, take another long drag, breathe out, and start mumbling again. Eventually, nothing remained of the cigarette but the filtered stub, which Sergei promptly flicked into the darkness. Adele looked down to see it smoldering against the heel of her boot.

"Got to take a piss."

Adele clenched her fists as the Russian strode toward the shrub, unzipped, and proceeded to relieve himself directly on the other side of the bush no more than a few feet from where she huddled. Sergei let out a satisfied groan as his urine stream struck the branches. His head fell back against his shoulders, allowing him to look up at the moonlit night sky. From somewhere deep within the island forest, the forlorn cry of an owl echoed across the waters of Rolf Cove. Sergei began to mimic the owl's call, chuckling to himself as he did so. This was followed by a shockingly loud blast of flatulence, which elicited even more laughter from the Russian.

Having fully emptied his bladder, the Russian turned, picked up the garbage sack, and began walking briskly up the narrow hiking path toward the bathrooms. Adele watched Sergei enter the second building on the north side furthest from the dock and then quickly reemerge, though this time he was holding a black garbage sack in his hand. He half jogged back down the trail with the sack swinging loosely at his side. Adele could hear his boots thumping against the dock planks. She moved out from behind the shrub in order to better see Sergei as he stepped onto the boat, watching as he disappeared inside.

Seconds later, the powerful engines roared to life and the boat pulled away from the dock with a noise that reminded Adele of a long line of Harley-Davidson motorcycles rumbling down a highway. Again, there were no navigation lights turned on to mark the vessel's path in the night. With its midnight-blue hull, the boat was nearly invisible as it returned into Canadian waters.

Adele stood up with a shake of her head as she realized how tightly wound the muscles of her body had become while she watched and waited for Sergei to leave. *Pretty sure that would qualify as too close for comfort.*

Another solemn hoot from the island owl sounded as Adele looked up at the bathroom where Sergei had left something behind. While she wasn't yet certain whom the bag was intended for, Adele was determined to confirm its contents. With a final glance down to the end of the dock to ensure she was alone Adele stepped onto the trail and carefully made her way in the darkness to the bathroom.

Once inside, she used the light on her phone to illuminate the small space's interior. There was no sign of the white garbage bag. The wood walls and floor remained bare. Adele looked up, hoping to spy a panel in the ceiling that might have been used to conceal the bag, but only saw more open space. She rapped the walls with her knuckles, trying to detect a hollow area, but found nothing to indicate where the bag could have been left. She proceeded to stomp on the floorboards but still found no evidence of a hiding place.

What the hell? Where did Sergei leave it?

Adele looked down at the circular, dark chasm that was the space beyond the surface of the toilet seat. *Oh, no.*

Though she didn't want to admit it, she knew the bag had to be somewhere inside the opening. She had looked everywhere else, and so if she were going to locate it, she would have to reach a hand into the toilet and feel around for the bag. Because Matia had no water system, the island's bathrooms were composting structures, meaning Adele was standing over what amounted to a large hole in the earth.

With a slightly trembling hand, she held her phone above the toilet opening and peered into the decomposing abyss while doing her best to forget the documentary she'd watched years earlier about hordes of giant rats thriving inside thousands of miles of sewage lines just beneath the city streets of New York. The phone's light revealed the composting pile of human waste several feet below but nothing else.

I'm not just reaching my hand in there and feeling around. No friggin' way.

Adele lowered her phone below the toilet seat, aimed it toward the side, and snapped a photograph. She then turned her hand so the camera faced the opposite direction and took another photo. Upon reviewing the second picture, she found what she was looking for. Hanging on a hook in the left corner beyond the toilet seat was the white trash bag. The distance from the surface was nearly three feet, meaning that if She were to successfully retrieve the bag, she would have to put her entire arm all the way to her shoulder into the darkest space beyond the opening.

She turned her head to the side and took a deep breath. Her face was locked into a tight-eyed grimace as her cheek pressed against the cold plastic toilet seat. She knelt down and put her arm into the hole. As soon as her fingers gripped the bag, she yanked it out with so much speed and force she fell backward against the door. With her heart thumping against her chest, Adele pushed herself up from the floor and opened the garbage bag to find a smaller green canvas duffel bag inside. She removed the second bag and discarded the first back down into the toilet opening.

The duffel bag felt relatively light. It made a distinct rattling noise while being moved into the crook of her left arm. Adele unzipped it with her other hand and found the bag stuffed with multiple unmarked plastic prescription bottles full of pills. The discovery of the pills confirmed at least part of the puzzle Adele hoped to soon put together.

Sergei is smuggling the pills in for Yuri Popov, using Matia as the drop point.

That left the critical question of who was then picking up the drugs Sergei was leaving on the island. Adele knew the answer to that remaining unknown would likely reveal itself soon enough.

It was only a matter of more waiting.

18

Adele had intended to remain on Matia for at least another day, hoping to discover who it was that showed up to take the bag left by Sergei. She awoke in the early morning hours to the realization that the weather had other plans. The previous day's blue sky had given way to ominous, dark-gray clouds and increasing wind, harbingers of yet another winter storm's imminent arrival. With temperatures dropping and the possibility of more snow, she decided it would be prudent to take the runabout back to Roche Harbor before worsening water conditions made that choice impossible.

The trip back, though relatively safe, was far from comfortable as waves crashed over the little boat's bow, leaving Adele soaked and shivering. It was with considerable relief that she rounded the corner that marked the entrance to Roche Harbor and made her way to her slip where she promptly tied up the runabout and returned to the warm and comforting confines of her sailboat residence where she intended to wait out the storm.

That wait didn't take long as the strong winds pushed the atmospheric disturbance north of the islands. By noon the wind decreased, and the temperatures warmed to an almost comfortable forty-two degrees. Adele took time to clean up and make herself something to eat. And then, after securing the bag of pills inside a locked cabinet hidden beneath one of the sailboat's cushioned bench seats, she returned outside to find Bryce Workman and Bob Tinnis talking to each other some forty feet farther down on the dock. The customs officer was scowling at the park ranger as Workman attempted to explain something to Bob in a voice too low for Adele to overhear.

Both men glanced at Adele as she stepped off the sailboat and onto the dock. Bob abruptly turned around and began walking toward the customs office, while the taller Workman gave Adele a happy smile and wave as he made his way to her. "Good morning, Ms. Plank! Say, was that you coming into the harbor early this morning?"

Adele zipped up her jacket and nodded. "Yeah, I suppose it was. I thought we agreed you would call me Adele."

Workman's smile widened further as he snapped his fingers together. "That's right! And you can call me Bryce."

The park ranger looked out at the harbor's still slightly agitated waters. "If you don't mind my asking, what would make a smart young lady like you risk going out on the water in this kind of weather? Are you working on another one of your newspaper stories?"

Adele looked more carefully at Workman's narrow face and noted the dark circles under his eyes. It appeared he hadn't been sleeping much of late. "I was about to ask you a similar question, Bryce. From where I was standing, it looks like your conversation with Mr. Tinnis wasn't improving his disposition any."

Bryce turned his head to look down the dock at the customs office. "Yeah, he's definitely a-cup-is-half-empty sort of fella. Speaking of bad moods, I want to apologize for how I acted during our last conversation. It had been a long day, and, well, I guess I might have taken it out on you a bit, and that wasn't fair of me to do."

"No need to apologize. If you do want to make it up to me, how about answering some questions?"

Bryce's smile, which Adele sensed was forced from the moment he saw her, collapsed. "Questions? I already told you. I don't want to be part of any newspaper story. I'm a government official and as such have to watch what I say."

"This isn't necessarily part of a story. Besides, I told you that I'm happy to keep your identity confidential regarding any information you do have to share that might later be used by me in an article."

The park ranger's mood continued to turn more defensive. He shook his head and backed away from Adele with hands held in front of him. "I told you I'm not interested in being involved in anything like that. I understand you have a job to do. I'm no different, but a big part of my job is knowing when to keep my mouth shut like any good servant of the taxpayers' dollar should do."

Adele stepped to the side, blocking Bryce from being able to move past her. "You didn't stay quiet when you told Sheriff Pine about that suspicious boat you saw docked a few nights back out at Matia, right?"

Bryce's eyes narrowed as the corners of his mouth dropped downward. "I was doing what the sheriff asked me to do, informing him of anything that might be out of the ordinary. That's the second time you've brought this subject up to me in a tone that I don't much care for, *Ms. Plank*."

"What tone is that, *Mr. Workman*?"

"A suspicious one. I don't like it. Not one bit."

Adele held her ground, thinking the angrier Bryce became, the more likely he might unintentionally give up more information. "Was Sheriff Pine the only one you informed of about the blue-hulled boat tied up to the dock at Matia?"

Bryce ran a hand over his head while looking back at the customs building. "Well, actually, I did let Bob know shortly after I called the sheriff. There's nothing odd about that, though. I mean, Lucas is the sheriff; I'm the park ranger. Bob runs the customs office here at the harbor. We're all basically law enforcement in one form or other, and the boat was a Canadian vessel, which makes my informing Bob all the more reasonable. Why do you ask?"

Adele shrugged, wanting to appear somewhat indifferent in order to continue convincing Workman she could be trusted. "Oh, I'm just trying to work out the timeline in my head. I'm also wondering if the only two who knew about that boat out there were you and Sheriff Pine. So was it right after you told the sheriff about the boat that you then told Mr. Tinnis as well?"

"I suppose," Bryce replied. "I mean, I don't know exactly how much time had passed, but I don't recall it being much." He glanced toward the customs office. "Say, are you worried Bob might be into some kind of trouble? He *has* been acting kind of strange lately, now that I think of it."

"Strange how?"

"Well, he seems—I don't know—a bit confused lately. Like something is on his mind. And there's that fall he said he took, the injury to his eye. He's always been a good man, so I'm not comfortable talking about him like this. I just thought I'd mention it to you."

"Thank you, Mr. Workman. I appreciate that. Have you heard anything more about the girl from Orcas Island who died?"

The abrupt transition to the subject of the teenage girl's death clearly rattled the park ranger as his gaze dropped to his shoes. "No, I haven't heard anything. What a terrible loss, though. What about you? Any news to report on how she died?"

Adele purposely exaggerated her look of surprise over Bryce not having already learned that drugs might have played a part. "You didn't know? The initial investigation suggests it was drug-related."

Bryce's hand covered his mouth. He appeared genuinely upset at being given that information. He shook his head slowly while fighting back tears. "Oh, I see. I imagine the sheriff is working very hard to find out if drugs were in fact the cause, and if so, where they came from."

"Yes, he is. Lucas is dealing with the passing of his father, of course, but knowing him, solving that case won't be far behind. There are concerns her death and Carl Blime's death might be related to illegal drugs coming into the islands by water."

Bryce straightened his narrow shoulders and looked down on Adele with one brow arched. "That's coming from the sheriff?"

"Unofficially, but yes, that seems to be where the investigation is going right now. I'm only telling you his information because, as you said, you're a law enforcement official as well."

Bryce ran a hand through his thin, yellow, straw-like hair. "That's right. We're all working on the same side. So does the sheriff think there could be more deaths related to these drugs he believes are coming in?"

"Without a doubt. Wherever they are coming from, there's no quality control. Each pill in the same bottle could be different, making them very dangerous to the people taking them."

Bryce took in a deep breath and then cleared his throat. "I see." He appeared to want to say more but then apparently changed his mind. He pointed toward the resort parking lot. "I have business in Friday Harbor I should be getting to."

Adele stepped to the side to allow him to pass. "Of course."

He took a few quick steps past Adele, stopped, and turned around. "Ms. Plank—Adele—if you hear anything more about the sheriff's investigation regarding those illegal drugs, please let me know. I would very much like to try and help."

"I'll do that as long as you do something for me."

Bryce used his thumb and forefinger to wipe at the corners of his mouth. "What would that be?"

Adele pointed toward the beach that marked the northeast border of the Roche Harbor marina, a narrow, three-hundred-foot-long space of sand and mud that was a favorite gathering spot for the many local island birds. Adele estimated they stood a little more than a hundred yards away from the beach, a span that was even closer than the distance from the entrance to Rolf Cove and the Matia public dock. "Can you tell me what kind of bird that is over there?"

A large, male great blue heron hunted the muddier section that was the beach's northern side. Its unmistakable white-and-black plume ran the length of its impressively beaked head. With the length of its sinewy neck fully extended, the long-legged bird stood nearly four feet tall.

Bryce's head turned as he strained to see the area where Adele continued to point. "I figured with you being a park ranger, you'd be the one I should ask," she said.

"While I appreciate your confidence in my knowledge of local flora and fauna, I'm afraid my eyes don't see nearly as far as they used to. I can make out *something* over there, but it's not much more than a blur from where I'm standing. Perhaps you could describe the bird to me."

Adele proceeded to do just that. Bryce quickly told her she was looking at one of the many herons that inhabited the island shores. As he readied to turn away and resume his trip back to the parking lot, Adele held up a finger.

"I'm sorry, just one more thing, Mr. Workman. I promise this is my last question for you—at least for today."

Bryce sighed, rolled his eyes, and then shrugged. "Go ahead. What is it?"

Adele cleared her throat, giving her time to plan her next words very carefully. "Well, the thing is, that's a rather large bird standing over there. I can see it clearly from here, but you can't, correct?"

Bryce issued another sigh. This one was louder and indicted his patience with Adele had expired. "You're being repetitive. I told you, I don't see from a distance as well as I used to. Give yourself a few more years and you'll understand."

Adele grinned as she wagged a finger at the park ranger. "You're absolutely right. I certainly don't fault you for being older than me and not being able to see as far. There's no *crime* in that!"

The park ranger's eyes narrowed at the mention of the word crime. He took a step toward Adele, his voice a near-whisper. "Get to your point."

"My point is that you told Sheriff Pine you saw that boat tied up at the Matia dock at night. There's no lighting on that dock. And the boat you say you saw has a dark-blue hull, making it almost impossible to see at night even for someone with excellent vision. You just admitted your own eyesight is far from excellent. Knowing that, how is it you came to see that boat while driving past Matia on what was an especially dark and stormy evening? The distance from the entrance to Rolf Cove and the Matia dock is greater than the distance from here to that blue heron. And yet even in daylight, you can't make out the details of that large bird over there. I can't help but wonder how your vision was somehow miraculously improved on that particular night?"

Bryce took another step toward Adele and stood over her with eyes blazing outrage. His tall, lean frame lent him an appearance very similar to that of the heron hunting smaller prey upon the nearby beach. "If you wish to make an accusation, come right out and say it. Otherwise, I think it best I leave before I lose my temper and do something I might regret."

"It isn't my intention to make you angry, Mr. Workman. I'm just looking for the truth."

The park ranger leaned down close enough to Adele that she could smell his coffee-drenched breath as it washed over her face. "Then you'd be smart to start looking somewhere else." He abruptly turned around and walked the entire length of the dock without looking back.

He didn't deny not actually seeing that boat out at Matia, Adele thought. *Now I have to figure out what would motivate him to lie.*

With a loud croaking squawk, the great blue heron spread its massive wings and took flight. Adele watched its slow labored departure as the large bird glided over the harbor's smooth saltwater surface, made a gentle turn to the left, and then flew directly over the US Customs and Border Protection office at the end of the dock.

Bryce Workman had just suggested Adele look for the truth somewhere else.

She decided to start there first.

19

Adele gave the door to the customs office a light knock, opened it, and was instantly hit by a blast of warm air pouring out from inside the small building. She entered the office and saw Bob Tinnis standing behind the counter, staring back at her. Despite the room's near-suffocating temperature, he wore a heavy winter jacket, and he'd covered his head with a black knit cap.

"Officer Tinnis, do you have a moment?"

Bob rubbed his forehead and groaned. "What do you want?"

"I had a few questions I was hoping you could help me with."

Bob took off the cap and ran a hand across what few remnants of short white hair remained on his head. "I'm not doing any interviews for that paper of yours, Ms. Plank. Your being here means Bryce ran you off already, and I'm just as apt to do the same."

"I assure you this is all off the record."

Bob grunted, giving Adele a look that indicated her assurances of their conversation remaining private meant little to him. "Nothing is *ever* off the record. A person says something to someone else—that's a record. I learned a long time ago it's best to just keep your mouth shut when people like you come around asking questions." He appeared to be using his hands to steady himself behind the counter as he let out a low, pained groan. He closed his eyes, pursed his lips, and took several deep, slow breaths.

"Are you okay?" Adele asked.

The customs officer opened his eyes and shook his head. Adele could see drops of sweat gathering on his forehead. "No, young lady, I am definitely *not* okay." He pushed a chair out from behind the counter and slowly lowered himself into it. Despite the sweat pouring down his face, he was shivering. With a shaking hand he pointed to the back room behind the counter. "Can you get me a glass of water from the sink, please?"

Adele walked into the low-lit room and filled a plastic cup with water, returned to the office's main room, and placed it into Bob's still-trembling hand. He put it to his lips, tilted his head back, and emptied it in one swallow. "Thank you. I tell you what. Go ahead and pull up a chair. I can't promise I'll give you anything that might resemble good conversation, though."

Adele moved a chair out from against the wall and sat down a few feet in front of Bob, who was wiping the sweat off his brow with the sleeve of his jacket. He noticed her watching him as he coughed into his hand. "Don't worry. I have no plans of dying just yet."

Adele wasn't so sure about that. His shivering appeared to be getting worse. "Do you need a doctor?"

Bob wrapped his arms around his chest, closed his eyes, and growled as his mouth formed a hard, grimacing line beneath his white mustache. When he spoke, the effort appeared to cause him considerable discomfort. "A doctor? That's the last thing I need. A doctor is who made me feel this way in the first place! Give it a minute. It'll pass. At least

I'm not puking anymore. Now, I just feel so weak and cold. I'm *always* cold since I cut back on those damn pills."

Adele's brows lifted at the customs officer's mention of pills. "What pills?"

Bob leaned to the side, reached into his right coat pocket, and withdrew a nearly empty prescription bottle. "*These* damn pills! I've been trying to get myself off them for the past two weeks. This is the last prescription I'm allowing myself to have. I've been on them for three years, and the doctor just keeps writing me another prescription for more. I'd tell him my hip was troubling me, and there you go—more pills. There have been days I can't even remember. Can you imagine? Entire days of my life are gone because I was so medicated. Well, my mind is made up. Enough is enough. I'd rather have my pain than the fog these things have turned my life into. I used to pop four of the little bastards a day. Now I'm down to just one, and when this bottle runs out, that's it. I'm done."

He wiped his nose and then held up two thick fingers. "I have two more years on this job, and I'll be damned if I end up a junkie in retirement."

Adele was suddenly thirsty, likely a result of the room's stifling heat. "You mind if I get myself some water?"

"Sure, help yourself," Bob said.

Adele was gone just a few seconds and then returned to her seat with a cup of water. Bob sat silently, watching her drink and waiting for her to finish before saying more. "I have to admit, for someone who told you I had nothing to say I sure unloaded a hell of a lot on you just then. Guess those words have been bottled up inside of me since I started my fight to push those pills away. Most people would have got right up and walked on out, but here you are."

"I don't scare easily," Adele replied with a shrug. "It's like I said when I came in. I have some questions I'm hoping you can help me with."

Bob cocked his head as he stroked his mustache. "And not a word of this goes in the newspaper, right? The last thing I need is more attention while I'm trying to straighten myself out. I can't risk losing this job. I'm sure the sheriff was wondering why I didn't allow them to draw my blood at the medical clinic. Well, now you know."

"This is all off the record. You have my word."

Bob held up the pill bottle. "Including what I just told you about my fight to get off these things?"

"Of course. I'm a reporter, not a gossip."

"I didn't think there was a difference."

Adele crossed her legs and folded her hands on her knee. "Where I'm concerned, there is."

With his trembling and profuse sweating having subsided, Tinnis glanced up at the low ceiling, rolled his head from side to side, and then shrugged "Okay, sure, why not? Ask your questions."

Adele waited for the customs officer's head to lower so she could look into his eyes.

He stared back at her and chuckled. "You're a confident little thing, aren't you?"

Adele ignored the compliment, choosing instead to proceed with her first question. "Did Bryce Workman tell you the other day about a blue-hulled boat that was docking out at Matia?"

"Yeah, but it wasn't the other day he mentioned that vessel to me."

Adele instinctively knew another potentially critical piece of information was about to be disclosed. "When did he first mention it?"

Bob had resumed stroking his mustache. "Oh, it was at least a few months ago. It was in the summer, right around the time you wrote the story about that poor Russian girl who was murdered. And he never mentioned anything about Matia. Did Bryce say something different to you about when he asked me about the boat?"

"He indicated to me it was just last week, around the same time he told Sheriff Pine the boat was out at Matia."

"I guess he got confused about that," Bob said with a frown. "Or maybe you heard him wrong."

Adele shook her head. "No, I didn't hear him wrong. He told me something that wasn't true."

"I've known Bryce Workman for a long time. He's a good guy who does his job and keeps to himself. He must have gotten the time mixed up or something. That's understandable given the stress he's been under."

"What stress is that?"

Bob looked away. "I don't want to share another man's troubles. In fact, he told me that information in confidence. Like I said, Bryce is a guy who mostly just keeps to himself."

Adele unfolded her legs and leaned forward. "Mr. Tinnis, what trouble is Bryce Workman in?"

Bob got up with a loud groan, grabbed his hip with one hand while pointing to the door with the other. "That's not for me to say. Why don't you go on and ask your friend Roland Soros about it? I'm sure he wouldn't mind explaining to you what he did to Bryce. And I'll tell you another thing. Bryce Workman could have shared that with a whole lot of people around here, but he chose not to. He's too proud. I don't see your newspaper reporting anything on *that*, but what I *do* see is it full of advertising I know Mr. Soros is paying for." Bob pointed at the door. "We're done here. You want to find out more about what the deal is between Roland Soros and Bryce Workman? You go bring it up with your rich friend. That story isn't mine to tell. Good day."

Adele closed the door behind her and gazed up at the Roche Harbor Hotel, inside of which the man Bob had contemptuously described as her "rich friend" was getting some much-needed rest. Even as she took her first steps toward the hotel, Adele's mind replayed the just-concluded conversation. It had further confirmed that Bryce Workman had lied both to her and Lucas about when he'd first seen Sergei's boat, but the reason for his telling that lie remained unknown. Had his intent been merely to mislead, or was the park ranger trying to accomplish something else?

When she reached the hotel Adele paused to look up at the balcony, expecting to find Tilda monitoring her arrival, but it was empty.

As she reached out to open the main entrance door, her mind repeated a question she was determined to soon have the answer to.

Roland, what the hell did you do to Bryce Workman?

20

"Yes, I know *exactly* why Mr. Workman is upset. He made it quite clear to me last year inside my office at the bank. I've been avoiding him ever since because, frankly, there's nothing I can do for him. The matter is completely out of my hands."

Roland's tone managed to be both defensive and apologetic. Adele had found him inside the hotel, playing cards with Brixton and Tilda, looking far more like his normally confident self. He was the picture of casual contentment in his navy-blue V-neck sweater, tan khakis, and dark leather penny loafers. He had greeted Adele with a wide smile, which Adele had not returned. Tilda had been quick to pick up on Adele's desire to speak with Roland alone and had risen from the table near the lobby fireplace and motioned for Brixton to follow her upstairs.

Adele sat down at the table across from Roland and explained how Bob Tinnis had suggested she ask him about Bryce Workman. The name caused Roland to grunt and shake his head, indicating it was a subject he would rather avoid. Adele persisted, wanting to know why the longtime San Juan County park ranger would be so angry with him. That was when Roland admitted to knowing what the reason was and had claimed there could be nothing done about it. Not satisfied with his attempt to push away her determination to learn more, Adele continued to demand an explanation.

"I'm not leaving here until you explain what took place between you and Mr. Workman. Bob Tinnis seems to think it's something that would have a whole lot of people around here upset if they were to learn of it."

Roland turned his face away, pretending to look at the beginnings of another cold winter rain shower outside. "It was *business*, Adele, and it was certainly not specific to Bryce Workman. I can't be responsible for people's inability to pay their debts. As you already know, I'm having a difficult enough time meeting my own financial obligations."

Adele grew impatient with Roland's obfuscation. "Roland, please answer my question. What happened between you and Mr. Workman?"

"Fine, I'll tell you the truth—not some one-sided gossip from the likes of Bob Tinnis."

Adele waited. Roland licked his lips, scanned the room to make certain no one else was nearby to overhear, and then began to speak. "My bank held the mortgage loan on his home. It was originally underwritten by my grandfather years earlier and then more recently approved by me for a cash-out refinance. We're a local bank; our business is built on a tradition of dealing almost exclusively with long-term residents, of which Mr. Workman is certainly one. About two years ago, when I began to put together what would become the Cattle Point project, I needed to find ways to increase my liquid assets. One of the easiest and quickest options available to me to do so was the packaging and sale of some of the smaller mortgages my bank was holding. Every year we get inquiries from various larger financial institutions, offering to purchase our mortgages from us, and every year, we turn those offers down."

Adele already sensed at least part of Roland's explanation. "Until recently."

Roland nodded. "That's right. Two years ago, I accepted what was a generous offer. Mr. Workman's mortgage was among those packaged and sold to another institution. It's common practice—perfectly legal. The fact is we're one of only a few small banks that continue to service almost all of our own mortgages throughout the life of the loan, even though there's significant profit to be made reselling those mortgages."

Adele knew there had to be much more than merely a resold mortgage to initiate the kind of ill will between Roland and Bryce Workman that Bob Tinnis indicated to her existed. Again, she allowed Roland time to gather his thoughts before he continued to further explain what had happened.

"What I didn't know is that Mr. Workman was facing serious financial hardship. Shortly after his loan was sold, he began falling behind on his payments. I assure you that I had no idea of this at the time. He later told me himself the morning he came screaming into my office at the bank, demanding I do something about it. I no longer owned his loan. There was nothing I could do. And before you or anyone else says I could have helped him, perhaps given him another loan, that's not how my business works. I can't endanger the bank's reserve funds to try and bail out every resident who might be dealing with financial troubles. My responsibility is to those who pay down their loans on time and those who qualify for loans in the future."

"Why did Mr. Workman refinance his original loan? What would he need that cash for?"

Roland's head lowered. His face went temporarily slack, devoid of emotion. When he looked up, he put an elbow on the table and placed the palm of his hand underneath his chin. "Your ability to get to the point, to the real issue, never ceases to amaze. That need for cash you just asked about is the root cause of the current mess Mr. Workman finds himself in. Apparently, he doesn't like to tell people about it. I'm not sure why he has been so secretive. Maybe it was the shame of his wife leaving him for someone else years ago. Or perhaps he didn't want attention put onto his daughter. Who really knows why people are the way they are? What I *do* know is that when I sold Mr. Workman's loan two years ago, I had no idea what he was dealing with at home. How could I? He never mentioned it. Not once."

"Workman has a daughter?"

Roland nodded. He continued to avoid looking directly into Adele's eyes. She took that as a sign of some underlying shame he felt regarding his own part in the story he was sharing with her.

"Yes," he said. "She's a teenager by now. The morning he came into my office, Mr. Workman told me his daughter had been diagnosed with a malignant form of multiple sclerosis five years earlier. He had already cashed out his retirement to pay the medical care for her that his insurance wouldn't cover. That's why he'd refinanced his mortgage—he needed to continue his daughter's treatment. Treatment he believes is the only thing keeping her alive."

Roland leaned over the table, his eyes pleading for understanding. "When Mr. Workman first refinanced the loan, I had no idea his reason for doing so. I didn't know anything about his daughter's medical condition. If I had, I promise you, I would never have packaged his loan to be sold."

"And yet, that's what happened because you were so motivated to try and get your Cattle Point project off the ground. Why didn't you extend Mr. Workman another loan, a line of credit?"

"I'm a business, Adele, not a charity. A bank doesn't extend credit to someone who has already proven an inability to pay. And you know what? Maybe if my Cattle Point project were already up and running, creating jobs, improving the local economy, and yes, *making a profit*, I would be in a better position to help someone like Bryce Workman."

If Adele's eyes had been guns, they were at that moment shooting bullets into Roland Soros. "You don't get to do that."

The look Roland shot back at Adele made clear he felt she was pushing him up against the proverbial wall. He chose to try and push back. "Do *what*?"

"Play the victim," Adele replied. "You're not the father with a daughter fighting for her life against a deadly disease. People around here come to you to make loans they believe will be kept local, not sold off to some financial conglomerate on the other side of the world. You just explained to me that was how your grandfather ran the bank. That was how he built his business, his reputation. Now your own greed and disloyalty to this community is destroying what your grandfather created—your family's legacy."

The words Adele spoke appeared to strike Roland in much the same way as a hand would have. His anger-reddened face flinched, and his nostrils flared. "You've had your say. That's enough."

"I wish that were true, Roland. I didn't come here to judge you about how you conduct your business, although I know that's how it feels to you. There's a much bigger and even more tragic component to this story unfolding right now."

Roland's eyes widened just as his anger dissipated and was replaced by curiosity. "What do you mean?"

Adele shook her head. "I can't share that with you yet."

Roland's lips pressed tightly together as he absorbed the implications of Adele's refusal. "But you *will* be talking to Lucas about it, right?"

Before Adele could respond, the sound of someone clearing their throat echoed through the hotel lobby. She turned around to see Tilda staring back at her.

"I am sorry to interrupt," Tilda said, "but we have guests arriving shortly for tomorrow's funeral service. If you two would like, you're welcome to continue your conversation in my private room upstairs."

Roland stood while shaking his head as he made his way toward the stairs. "We're done here. I don't wear a badge, so she doesn't have anything more to say to me. I'll just grab my things and be on my way back home, Ms. Ashland. Thank you for allowing me to stay. I feel much better having been your guest. Please extend my best wishes to Mr. Bannister. I hope he gets to make that film. Tell him how much I enjoyed getting to know him. It's not every day you play cards with an actor the rest of the world presumes is dead. Oh, and let him know his secret is safe with me."

When Roland's foot rested upon the first step of the stairs, he paused to look back at Adele. "I understand it's your job, Adele—all this investigative reporting work. I've been encouraging you to pursue that since you first came to these islands. I just hope there doesn't come a time when what we both do for a living gets in the way of what we could be to each other."

Both Adele and Tilda listened to Roland's footsteps as he resumed his departure upstairs. Adele could feel Tilda's eyes on her and awaited the inevitable inquiry.

"It appears you struck a nerve," Tilda said.

"Yeah, I seem to have that effect on people."

Tilda sat in the same seat Roland had just vacated. She gave Adele a wide smile as she looked at her with eyes glimmering mischievous approval. "Well, of course, my young, intrepid reporter, all the great ones do."

21

Dr. Edmund Pine's memorial service took place inside the little white hillside chapel that had served the people of Roche Harbor for more than a century. The chapel's construction was originally ordered by Roche Harbor's founder, John McMillan, a lawyer-turned-business-magnate islander who had wanted to provide a place of worship for his and other families who came to work and live as part of the emerging, late-nineteenth-century seaside community.

The structure housed just six rows of hand-painted wood bench seats divided down the middle by a narrow walkway that led to the small altar area at the front where the doctor's gold-colored urn sat atop the podium. Next to that was a large photograph of Edmund and Katarina Pine, with a smiling Lucas dressed in his high school football uniform, standing between them, an arm resting on the shoulders of both his mother and father. A number of stained-glass windows allowed just enough late-morning light into the space to push back the gloom and allow those inside to see around them more clearly.

"There won't be too many people here. My understanding is Dr. Pine had made it clear to Lucas he didn't want a large service—just a quick hello-and-goodbye sort of thing. Speaking of which, I haven't actually seen Lucas here, have you?"

Adele shook her head. She sat next to Suze Blatt, the perpetually cheerful, middle-aged owner of the Friday Harbor bookstore and one of the first in the islands to warmly welcome Adele into the community nearly three summers ago. As soon as Suze had spotted Adele making her way up the steep church steps, she'd called out her name and demanded a hug, remarking it had been much too long since they had last spoken to each other and demanding they sit together for the service.

Once inside the church, Suze proceeded to provide Adele with a verbal accounting of everyone who arrived, including personal histories, rumors, and general public standing. "That is an old fishing buddy of Dr. Pine's from way back. He moved away, oh, it must have been nearly ten years ago. And that attractive older woman there used to head the county personnel office. She works down in Olympia now, state government stuff. That distinguished gentleman, hmmm, I think he might be a professor from Bellingham. Normally see him around here during the summer months. Of course, you already know Gunther Fox and Chancee Smith, the sheriff's deputies. And there is Councilman Joe Box, and that is Edmund's nurse, Maxine. Oh, the poor dear, she looks so upset."

And so went Suze's commentary until eventually, she was interrupted by the arrival of Avery and Bess Jenkins. Adele noted how heavily Avery leaned on his wife's arm and tried to hide his badly trembling hands. Suze immediately slid down the bench seat and motioned for the older couple to sit down.

"Avery, you shouldn't have walked all those church steps in your condition! We don't want to be having two funerals on the same day!"

Though the remark was well intentioned, Avery's deep scowl indicated he didn't care for it. He pointed to a copy of the Bible placed in a slot at the back of the bench in front of them. "There's a book for you to read, Suze. See if you remember how to do it *silently*."

Bess lightly nudged her husband with an elbow. His shoulders slumped as his face took on the appearance of a scolded Basset Hound. "I'm sorry, Suze. You didn't deserve that."

She gave both Suze and Adele light hugs before helping Avery as he carefully lowered himself into his place at the end of the bench where he then promptly appeared to be falling asleep. Bess leaned to her right to whisper to Adele. "I knew this would be too much for him, but he insisted. It took us almost ten minutes just to get up those steps. Suze is right, you know. It about killed the stubborn old goat."

Avery opened one eye to glare at his wife. "I may be stubborn, and I may be old. But I'm not yet deaf!"

Bess chuckled and gave Avery a quick peck on the cheek, happy to see him energetic enough to play ornery.

Adele saw Suze's eyes suddenly widen. She followed the bookstore owner's gaze and watched as Roland Soros, accompanied by Tilda, took a seat at the very back of the church. He was dressed in an immaculately tailored black suit and tie, the epitome of island-mogul success. *He might be fooling the others here,* Adele thought, *but I know better.*

With brows lifted over her thick-lens glasses, Suze continued her conversation with Adele. "He certainly cuts quite a dashing figure, doesn't he?"

Adele didn't answer, instead wondering about Lucas's ongoing absence from his father's memorial just as a bent-backed, white-haired pastor dressed entirely in black strode into the church, carrying, of all things, a guitar. He leaned the guitar against a wooden chair at the front of the church and then took his place behind the podium.

The pastor looked out from beneath heavy lids at the small gathering seated before him and proceeded to read aloud in a voice that was both soft yet commanding, a passage from the Bible. "For everything there is a season, and a time for every matter under heaven: a time to be born, and a time to die; a time to plant, and a time to pluck up what is planted. Amen."

The pastor gripped both sides of the podium and cleared his throat. "I am not a resident of these beautiful islands that Edmund Pine loved so much and happily served for so many years, but we were close friends once. As time went on and our lives became their own, we remained acquaintances via letters written to each other during anniversaries, birthdays, and holidays. He would seek my counsel from afar, and I was all too happy, and honored, to give it. Edmund was a beloved father, husband, and friend to so many on these islands. As most of you here today know, he had such a gift for caring and healing until his own sickness took that ability from him. It is a terribly cruel thing to see a great mind slipping away, day by day, week by week, until so little of the person that was remains."

Several people flinched as a great cannon-blast of thunder from outside shook the chapel floorboards. The pastor glanced up at the ceiling before continuing. "Edmund loved many things in his life, but there were two things he loved most above all else: The first was his beautiful wife, Katarina, taken from him much too soon by a stroke. The second, of course, is Edmund's son and only child, Lucas. And it has been Lucas who returned to these islands to care for his father following his mother's death, the act of a good and loving child."

The pastor had to raise his voice to be more heard over the deluge of emerging rainfall outside. "In his final letter to me just three months ago, Edmund reminded me of a time when I stayed at his home during a Fourth of July weekend many years earlier. Lucas was still just a little thing, and both Edmund and Katarina were healthy, happy, and in love. That was one of the more interesting things about his disease. Edmund struggled to recall his own immediate yesterdays, while finding it far easier and comforting to recount details from decades earlier. It was during that weekend Edmund and his wife managed to surprise me so much that I found it difficult to grasp what I was both seeing and hearing. It was a thing so unexpected, so seemingly out of place and out of character from the man I thought I knew. Granted, I had seen Edmund play guitar before. He was self-taught as a teenager and had become skilled enough to play and sing the music of our own youth. Songs like Ricky Nelson's "A Little Too Much" and Bobby Rydell's "Kissin' Time." Well, on that particular Fourth of July, I came to learn that Katarina, who had always been something of an adventurous soul that was made more so by a remarkable singing voice, had helped to develop in her husband an appreciation of *all* music."

Suze put a hand to her mouth. "I remember this. I remember what he's talking about. The talent show!"

Adele heard murmurs of recognition from others in the church as well while the rain outside transitioned fully from showers to a downpour.

The pastor nodded and smiled. "Ah, I see some of you recall that day as well. It was the local talent show. It was on a little outdoor stage just above the Friday Harbor marina where I watched my friend show an entirely different side of himself to the community he served. Edmund played the guitar, Katarina sang, and little Lucas danced at their side. All of you who were fortunate enough to have been there to see it were most likely just like me with your mouths hanging open, shocked and thoroughly entertained by that remarkable and most unexpected performance."

The pastor held up a white envelope. "In this letter, likely written during one of his last moments of mental clarity, Edmund Pine made two final requests of me: The first was to do what I'm doing now—presiding over what he demanded was to be an intimate and *brief* remembrance. He stated how he hated going to long funerals and didn't want to put others through that same experience. Besides, he was certain Katarina would be waiting, and he didn't wish to delay that reunion any more than he had to."

Adele fought back tears and failed, recalling the walk she had taken last summer with Lucas and his father to visit Katarina's gravesite within the beautiful, wooded solitude of the Roche Harbor cemetery. She looked down to see Suze giving her hand a reassuring squeeze as the pastor continued.

"The second request was for me to convince Lucas to play the song his father and mother played together on that wonderfully warm Friday Harbor Fourth of July all those years ago—the same song that won them first place at the talent show. You see, Lucas learned to play and sing as well, taught to do so by both his talented parents. I don't believe he advertised it much. Perhaps he thought it didn't fit with the athletic skills for which he would later and rightfully earn so many accolades. Edmund assured me Lucas knows the song because they all three played and sang it together in their home for years after that winning Fourth of July performance. It apparently remained one of Katarina's most treasured memories. And so it became for Edmund as well. I don't think Lucas will mind my telling you he initially refused the request. After some thought, though, and with a few days to understandably process the loss of a loved one, he has agreed to play and sing it this one last time. I know Edmund will be watching, and it will please him greatly. He also mentioned in the letter his hope that a young woman whose name he could not recall would be here today as well so that she might see there is much more to his son than he might be willing to show her on his own."

Several hushed gasps rose up from among the gathering as Lucas suddenly appeared from behind a curtained doorway that was to the right of the podium. He wore his sheriff's uniform and walked slowly toward the chair against which the guitar rested. This time Suze brought both hands to her mouth as tears began to fall down her face with the same intensity as the rain that fell upon the chapel roof.

"Oh, my goodness this is just . . ." The bookstore owner was actually at a loss for words, leaving Adele to wonder what all the fuss was about.

Lucas sat in the chair and placed the guitar across his lap, keeping his head down to avoid looking at the people seated directly in front of him. Adele heard him sniffle, then clear his throat. "Uh, I want to thank you all for coming today. My father was a great man not because he did great things but because those things he did do, he did with love, compassion, and respect for others. I also want to thank Pastor Jerry Marks for the prayer and the kind words. My dad, well, I know he would have approved."

Adele heard the struggle in Lucas's voice as he fought to maintain his composure, like a string being stretched to its breaking point. Several people flinched in their seat as a booming thunderclap caused the church windows to rattle.

"It's true what Pastor Jerry said," Lucas continued. "I didn't want anything to do with playing any music, let alone in front of all of you. Then I remembered that Fourth of July and how amazed the people around here were when they heard my mom and dad singing together. That was my parents. They were always full of surprises. It was one of those perfect moments in your life you wish you could return to again and again. And even though we can't ever really go back, we can try and remember so we can keep that memory alive. I realized that for my dad, who in the end had to fight so hard to remember anything, to remember that day, that song, it must have really meant a lot to him. He played the guitar, and my mother sang the words. Now they're both gone and I'm left to try and do alone what we once all did together. I don't sing nearly as well as my mom, or play guitar like my dad, but I'll do my best."

The only son of Edmund and Katarina Pine looked up for the first time since entering the church. "Okay, here goes . . . something."

Lucas closed his eyes, took a deep breath, and then slammed his pick down against the guitar strings, creating a wall of acoustic sound that managed to rival the thunder and rain outside. With each chord played, with each verse spoken, Lucas suddenly appeared to Adele as something far greater than the mere sum of his already impressive parts.

It was a song titled "Don't Let Us Get Sick" by the artist Warren Zevon. Adele vaguely remembered it on the radio in the days of her own youth but could not recall any song at any time impacting her as deeply and profoundly as Lucas's rendition did inside that church as the storm raged outside. He sang of the passage of time, the fear of death, and the hope that those you love will live on and find happiness without you. It was a moment in which Adele witnessed Lucas letting go, however briefly, of all his carefully constructed defenses. As he sang one lyric and then the next, his voice sometimes cracking, his eyes tightly closed, Lucas revealed the anger, the fear, and the unrelenting determination to push beyond the expectations of others and more importantly, those he continued to impose upon himself.

It was beautiful.

Adele watched through her own tears and knew she could no longer deny the truth—she was falling in love.

Once the song ended, Lucas put the guitar down and got up. He again thanked everyone for coming and watched silently from the front of the chapel as people filed out. Adele said goodbye to Suze, Avery, and Bess, and even gave Roland a quick nod before he and Tilda made their way down the stairs until, finally, only Lucas and Adele still remained inside the church.

"I'm going to bury my dad's urn, and then we can meet to discuss the case. There have been some new developments I want to get you up to speed on."

Adele, still stunned by Lucas's performance, stood near the door saying nothing until she realized with a start that he expected her to answer. "Yes, that's good. I have something I need to show you as well."

Lucas cocked his head. "You find something out?"

Adele nodded, forcing herself to return to reporter mode as she recalled the drugs she had taken from Matia that were still being kept hidden on her sailboat. "Yeah, I did. It's important."

Lucas appeared to be contemplating having the discussion on the investigation right there. Adele knew he needed true closure regarding his father's death and didn't want to be the cause of any delay. "Did you want me to come with you to the gravesite?" she asked.

Lucas disappeared behind the curtain, calling out no as he did so. When he reemerged, he held a shovel over his left shoulder and picked up his father's urn with his other hand. "Thanks for the offer, but I won't be long. I'll see you soon."

Carrying the shovel and his father's remains, Lucas moved through the door and was soon well down the path heading toward the forest cemetery and his mother's grave. Adele stood watching his departure from the top of the church steps until he finally disappeared into the trees, seemingly intent at least for a moment longer to be alone with only his loss and pain to keep him company.

A beam of sunlight broke through the clouds, illuminating the path Lucas had just taken, while in the distance a great multicolored rainbow marked both an ending and a new beginning over the waters of Roche Harbor.

22

Where is he?

Before leaving for the graveyard, Lucas had informed Adele he would see her soon. That had been nearly three hours ago. Adele tried to call Lucas's cell phone, but like the previous four attempts, it went directly to voice mail. She texted him numerous times but had yet to receive a reply.

By the time the sheriff's delayed return moved well into its third hour, Adele decided she could no longer simply sit inside her sailboat, watching as daylight turned to darkness. She put on her running shoes, slipped into a light jacket, and took off down the dock to see what had become of Lucas.

Adele first looked in the parking lot, where she confirmed the sheriff's SUV remained parked near the hotel. The sight of the vehicle caused a worried tightening in Adele's throat. Her jog to the cemetery was accompanied by darkening skies. With eyes locked in front of her, Adele pushed herself to move faster. When she saw the white hand-painted sign marking the entrance to the cemetery, Adele bounded up the path that led farther into the forested burial grounds.

There!

It was Katarina Pine's grave. A small section of freshly upturned earth marked the spot where Lucas had buried the urn. The shovel the sheriff had taken with him lay next to the grave. Adele knelt down and scanned the area, looking for any clue as to where Lucas might have gone. There appeared to be no sign of a struggle or indication of any injury. She stood up and began to walk in slow circles around the gravesite, extending the circle outward as she went, carefully looking for any indication of what might have caused Lucas to drop the shovel and then seemingly vanish.

The toe of Adele's shoe hit against something heavy. She looked down, brushed away some leaves, and blinked several times, hoping her eyes were playing tricks. *Oh, no.*

Adele reached out and very carefully picked up the sheriff's gun, surprised by how heavy it felt in her hands. The troubling discovery left no doubt.

Lucas was in trouble.

Thoughts of the sheriff lying dead somewhere invaded Adele's mind. She promptly forced them out. *Remain calm, Adele. Think this through. Look around and see what needs to be seen. The shovel is dropped, the gun is dropped, but the ground isn't disturbed. Lucas is a big guy. If he was knocked out and dragged somewhere, there would be a trail left behind. If there had been a struggle, the ground would be more disturbed. That means someone most likely snuck up on him. They had to have been armed, told Lucas to drop his weapon, and then took him. The question is where—and why?*

Adele removed her phone from her coat pocket, intending to call the sheriff's office and inform Samantha Boyler that Sheriff Pine had gone missing. Before she could press the first number, the phone's ring tone sounded, startling her so badly she almost dropped the device. She looked down to see it was Lucas calling.

With relief washing over her, Adele gazed up at the canopy of trees, and with a wide smile on her face, put the phone to her ear. "Do you have any idea how freaked out I've been looking for you?"

A muffled male voice that did not belong to Lucas, answered. The conversation was slow and deliberate, as if each word was carefully considered prior to being spoken. "Listen carefully. You took something that was not yours. This has upset the balance of power on the islands. I *must* have it returned. If not, the sheriff dies. Do not seek help from anyone else. Not the sheriff's deputies. Not your friends. No one. Do you understand?"

Adele knew the call was about the pills she had taken from Matia. She answered immediately. "Yes. Do you have Sheriff Pine? How do I know he's still alive?"

"Do what I say, and I won't kill him."

Adele put her hand over the phone and looked around, trying to determine whether she was being watched. The woods made no sound, remaining as quiet as the cemetery occupants themselves. She returned the phone to her ear. "Tell me what you want me to do."

There was a prolonged pause. Adele feared the call had been ended or that she had lost the signal. "I said—"

The muffled voice returned. "Do you have the bag?"

Adele realized then the person wasn't actually certain she was the one to take the drugs from Matia. She considered lying. The weight of Lucas's gun in her pocket made her reconsider. The sheriff was out there somewhere, unarmed, being held captive—or worse.

"Yes. I have the bag."

"Go to the Orcas Island watchtower. Leave the bag on the observation deck. You have two hours. Go alone. Speak of this to no one. Any delay, any deviation from these very simple instructions, and you never see the sheriff again. Tell me you understand."

Adele gritted her teeth, the result of the effort it took to keep her voice calm. "I understand."

"Good. Two hours, Ms. Plank. It's nearly 5:00 p.m. The sheriff's life is now being measured in those remaining two hours. Tick-tock."

The call ended.

Adele knew the last ferry from Friday Harbor to Orcas Island left at 5:30. She had just over thirty minutes to return to her sailboat, grab the bag, get to her car, and make the drive to Friday Harbor.

It's not enough time.

Time enough or not, Adele knew she had no choice but to try. She began to move and then stopped. The sheriff's gun remained in her pocket. Knowing it would slow her down she placed it next to the tombstone of Lucas's mother and lightly covered it with leaves.

Adele ran.

Arms and legs moved in unison. Trees flashed beside her in blurred hues of browns and greens. She focused on her breathing, each inhale and exhale echoing in her ears, drowning out the sound of her shoes hitting the hard-packed dirt and gravel path. When she thought she could go no faster, she did.

The white-and-green outline of Tilda's hotel loomed ahead, marking Adele's arrival at the marina. If Tilda watched from her balcony, Adele didn't know and didn't care. Her eyes remained locked on the path directly in front of her. Her feet hit the dock and kept going, each stride marking her progress with a thump-thump-thump sound as she sped to her slip.

By the time Adele was inside the sailboat, her shirt was soaked in sweat. She grabbed the bag, clutched her keys, and emerged back onto the dock, already running toward the parking lot. After throwing the bag onto the MINI's passenger seat, she jammed the key into the ignition, and started the car. It was 5:13 p.m.

Go!

With a squeal of tires, the MINI catapulted itself from the parking lot toward the main road. The last of the winter-afternoon light was all but gone, requiring Adele to turn on the headlights. In much the same way as when she was running in the woods, her eyes scanned the road directly ahead and ignored all else. Stop signs were treated as suggestions. Cars in front of her were passed. The MINI's small engine let out an angry whine, its tachometer moving into the red as Adele downshifted into a corner, then mashing the accelerator and up-shifting when the road straightened out. She had never considered herself a particularly skilled driver, but on this day, with Lucas's life threatened,

Adele proved better than most.

It was 5:27 when the MINI entered the outskirts of Friday Harbor. The ferry terminal was another mile away. A speed-limit sign indicated thirty-five miles per hour. Adele passed it doing more than seventy.

As the clock turned to 5:28, Adele had just two thoughts. The first was to arrive at the ferry terminal on time. The second was to make certain she didn't hit anyone while doing so.

There it is.

The terminal's parking lot was empty. The departing vehicles were already loaded.

The ferry horn hasn't blown yet. It's still there.

The little car became temporarily airborne as Adele catapulted over a large speed bump. The vehicle's bumper guard crashed against the pavement with a great metallic shriek that sent sparks flying out from underneath both sides of the hood as Adele fought to maintain control and steer the vehicle toward the still-docked ferry.

"Hey! Lady! What the hell?" A yellow-vested ferry worker waved his arms wildly as Adele drove by him. He was in his early twenties, clean-shaven with short-cut blond hair and acne-plagued skin. He was clearly upset over Adele's high-speed arrival.

A blast from the ferry horn caused Adele to slam on the brakes. With the car still running, she got out, yelling at the ferry worker while pointing to the soon-to-be departing vessel. "I need to get on! This is an emergency."

The ferry worker put his hands on his hips and shook his head. "Sorry, it's pulling out. Looks like you're going to have to come back in the morning."

Adele felt as if a vein in her skull was about to burst. She shouted her refusal to accept the ferry worker's terms. "No! You don't understand. *I'm getting on that boat.*"

With eyes lit by unrelenting determination, Adele returned to her car, slammed the door, and accelerated toward the ferry's steel docking platform. The ferry worker cried out for her to stop. She could see him waving his arms as he unleashed an explosion of expletives.

Right back at you, buddy.

Another yellow-vested man emerged from inside the ferry, looking confused by Adele's sudden arrival. He was older than his coworker by a good twenty years, with a brown-and-gray beard and large belly that hung over the belt of his jeans.

Adele rolled down her window and honked her car's horn. "Please, I have to get on the ferry!"

The older ferry worker scowled as he shook his head and then motioned for Adele to back her car up away from the platform that connected the ferry vessel to the dock. Adele answered with a second honk of the horn and leaned her head out the window. "Sir, I'm getting on."

The younger of the two male ferry workers stood in front of Adele's car with his feet shoulder-width apart and demanded she back up. Adele responded with another honk.

"Lady, if you don't get that car out of here, I'm calling the sheriff."

The irony of the ferry worker's threat only further enraged Adele. She was running out of time. With an exasperated growl she flung open her car door and confronted the young ferry worker, her voice trembling with fury. "Get the hell out of my way. This is an emergency."

The man was about to respond when a female voice inquired from directly behind him. "What's going on here?"

The woman who arrived was older, nearly sixty. She was of average height and build, with shoulder-length blonde-gray hair, a prominent nose, and intelligent, hawk-like eyes that darted left and right, quickly assessing the situation. The two male ferry workers stood shoulder to shoulder. The younger one pointed a thumb at Adele.

"This lady comes flying in here, demanding to be let on. I told her to turn around. She won't listen. Says it's an emergency. That's the same thing the ones running late always say, am I right? It's *always* an emergency."

The female ferry worker, who Adele could tell was the one in charge, stepped forward to give Adele a more thorough looking over. She wore a nametag that indicated her name was Anna Davidson. The woman's eyes narrowed slightly.

"You're the reporter. The name is Adele, right?"

Adele nodded. She had never been more grateful to have been recognized. "I am. Please, Anna, I need you to believe me when I say this is an emergency. I have to get to Orcas Island now."

The young ferry worker scoffed. "Can you believe this crap? Look, lady—"

Anna cut him off, her tone making it clear he was done talking. "Shut up, Mike."

Mike's mouth abruptly closed while his face reddened. "Is this about a story for the paper?" Anna asked.

Adele could feel the time slipping away. It was maddening. "If I don't get to Orcas, I'm afraid it will be."

The two women's eyes locked, each taking a measure of the other. After several seconds of intense silence, Anna took a step back and motioned toward the ferry. "I believe you believe that. Welcome aboard, Adele."

Once she was safely on the ferry and moving with a handful of other cars toward Orcas Island, Adele's hands slipped from the steering wheel of her car. She looked down to see them shaking as the realization of just how close she had come to being stranded in Friday Harbor took hold.

Her eyes closed. *We're gonna make it. Lucas will be fine. I got this.*

Adele's eyes opened. She glanced at the clock.

5:41 p.m.

She had an hour and twenty minutes to keep Lucas Pine alive.

23

The Orcas Island watchtower was located at the peak of Mount Constitution, the highest point in all of the San Juan Islands. Rising up from the nearly five-thousand-acre Moran State Park, Mount Constitution stands watch over the region from its vantage point some twenty-four hundred feet above the shoreline.

The tower was first constructed nearly a century earlier during the Great Depression. It was built using material obtained from the multiple sandstone quarries that once dotted the largest of the San Juan Islands. The fifty-foot-high structure, which would have looked right at home protecting the gates of a Medieval castle in Europe, contains several small, cell-like rooms and a series of stone steps leading to the tower's observation deck, once used by the forest service to watch for wildfires during the warm summer months. It is from there that visitors can look out at all of the major and minor surrounding islands, and at the contrasts of dark-green water, brown-and-gray shorelines, and lush green forests. In the east looms Mount Baker, and when the skies are clear, one can see as far as Mount Rainier to the south, two majestic, snow-capped titans that are still active volcanic remnants of the region's chaotic geological past.

Even during daylight hours, the narrow, switchback road up to the tower requires a slow and careful ascent. Accidents are not uncommon. On this night, both daylight and time were luxuries Adele didn't have the benefit of. With the MINI's high-beams lighting the way, her foot mashed down the accelerator, pushing the car as quickly up the cliff-side road as possible without losing control and plummeting several hundred feet down to the rocks below.

The MINI's tires screamed in protest. Adele grimaced, spinning the steering wheel to the left and then frantically corrected the car's direction by jerking the wheel back to the right. *You can't save Lucas if you die on the way there, Adele. Keep this thing on the road.*

The clock read 6:44 p.m.

The ferry ride from Friday Harbor to the Orcas Island ferry dock was nearly forty minutes. The drive from one side of Orcas Island to the other and then through Moran State Park and up the twisting road to the top of Mount Constitution normally took travelers an hour. Adele had no choice but to try and make it in considerably less time.

Large, heavily knotted limbs from the ancient evergreen and pine trees that dominated the park reached across the road. It made driving the already narrow road feel even more suffocating, dangerous, and difficult. For Adele, the worst part was not being able to see the great chasm she knew was just off the side of the paved mountain path. The darkness above was matched by an even greater inky black below. She couldn't help but imagine the MINI sliding off the road, followed by a moment of seeming weightlessness. There would be the roar of wind, the sensation of falling, and then the terrible and final impact of metal upon earth, water, and stone.

6:49 p.m.

Thoughts of her own safety were pushed aside as Adele refocused on reaching the watchtower in time. Her eyes squinted at the blur of road and forest ahead. One hard turn was followed by another and yet another. The headlights illuminated a white-and-green sign:

Tower: 2.4 miles.

6:52 p.m.

The road's steep incline had flattened out and what appeared to be a long straightaway was just ahead. Adele engaged the clutch, slammed the gearshift down, and pushed the accelerator to the floor.

Another hard turn suddenly appeared, and beyond that, Adele was certain, a long fall to death. One hand spun the wheel left, while the other hand downshifted.

The car's tires began to slip.

Adele's eyes went wide as the squeal of pavement was replaced by the crunch of dirt and gravel as the car slid sideways. *I'm going over.*

Adele accelerated.

She had meant to slam on the brakes, but in her panic, with disaster looming no more than a few feet from the vehicle's back tires, she accidently pushed down on the gas pedal.

The whine of the MINI's motor combined with that of the wheels sliding across the gravel. It was at that moment a most fortunate thing happened. With the added acceleration and power, the tires dug in and pushed the car forward back onto the road and away from the abyss. Adele hit the brakes, bringing the MINI to a full stop. The hands that gripped the wheel shook violently. Her breath came in short gasps. Sweat covered her face.

6:54 p.m.

After taking a deep breath, Adele put the car into gear and resumed making her way as quickly as possible to the tower. She could see a single light illuminating the rock and mortar structure. No other vehicles occupied the parking lot.

Adele came to a screeching halt, grabbed the duffel bag, and flung open the car door. She nearly fell when her toe stubbed an uneven section of the concrete walkway that led to the tower. She cried out in the darkness, regained her footing, and then continued running with the bag slung over her shoulder.

A phone began to ring.

Adele, standing at the watchtower's entrance, looked up.

A second ring confirmed the noise was coming from the observation deck. Adele bolted into the tower, located the stone steps, and began to run, holding her cell phone out in front of her to help light the way. The stairwell was like a coiled snake leading upward. By the fourth ring, Adele was taking the steps three at a time, her thighs and calves burning from the effort. She ignored the pain.

Don't stop ringing!

As she reached the observation deck, there was a sixth ring. Adele feared it would be the last. Her eyes scanned the stone floor, the wall, every nook and cranny she could find.

There!

Lying against the wall just four steps away was a black plastic flip phone. Adele scrambled to pick it up. "Hello!"

Silence answered.

"I'm here! I have the bag." Adele thought she might have heard breathing. "Hello?" There was the sound of scuffling, another breath, and then a throat clearing. Finally, she heard the same muffled voice as before.

"That was close, Ms. Plank. I started to worry you weren't going to make it."

Adele held the phone to her ear while looking down to the area directly below the observation deck, trying to make certain the voice on the other end wasn't out there somewhere watching her. "Well, I *did* make it. I'll leave the bag here just like you asked as soon as you tell me where Lucas is."

"If you hope to see the sheriff unharmed, you'll need to hurry yet again, Ms. Plank. You'll find him in the place you just left him."

Adele's eyes narrowed. "What?"

"He's at the cemetery in Roche Harbor—the mausoleum."

Adele thought she heard the shuffle of a shoe over stone. She spun around, held her breath, and listened. The tower was silent.

"Wait, you don't have him? Where are you?"

"Hurry, Ms. Plank. Leave the bag and go. The clock is ticking once again for your friend the sheriff."

The call ended.

Adele dropped the bag, put both the flip phone and her own phone into her pocket, and then made her way slowly down the stairs, uncertain whether or not she was still alone in the tower. With each step taken, she feared a hand or face would suddenly emerge from the darkness. Once at the tower's base, she stood next to the doorway and peered into the gloom beyond, looking for any sign of danger. She had left the MINI running and was grateful to hear the idle of its engine.

Sprint to the car, lock the doors, and get the hell out of here.

Adele took a moment to try and see any threat waiting for her outside. There was no wind. The trees stood still. The still-idling MINI awaited her return.

With a soft grunt, Adele took off running into the night. She reached her car, opened the door, slammed it shut, and hit the lock button. A quick glance into the rearview mirror indicated nothing moved behind her, while the headlights revealed the path ahead appeared to be safe as well.

Adele drove from the parking lot to the road where she began to make her way quickly, though this time much more safely, down the mountain. She was nearly halfway back to the Moran State Park entrance when she slowed down and then stopped. Adele sat in the MINI on the side of the road and realized she wouldn't be able to leave the island. There was no ferry service until morning. Whoever the voice was who had sent her scurrying all the way from Roche Harbor to the top of Orcas Island's Mount Constitution, had overlooked that fact. They needed her gone from Orcas so they could pick up the bag of drugs without being discovered, and they were using her concern for Lucas's safety to get her back to Roche Harbor—and away from them.

The car's clock read 7:35 p.m.

I need some help.

Adele called Roland. The conversation was brief. She didn't want any more time wasted. She put the phone down, turned the wheel, and sped back up the mountain toward the observation tower.

Adele was now almost certain who she would find picking up the bag. In this mystery of illegal drugs, death, and deception, she had allowed herself to be played by someone else's rules.

She was now determined to start playing by her own.

24

A quarter mile before reaching the watchtower, Adele pulled off into a campsite area that allowed her to park the MINI some fifty yards from the road where it would be well hidden by both darkness and trees. She kept the car running to keep herself warm but shut off the lights and waited. Her mind replayed the evidence she had already uncovered, applied that knowledge to potential suspects, and then once again came to the same conclusion regarding who she believed would be coming for the drugs she had left inside the tower.

The phone in her jacket pocket began to vibrate. It was Roland. Nearly an hour had passed since she had called him and asked that he get to the Roche Harbor mausoleum as quickly as possible to see if Lucas was there. "I found him. He's groggy but okay. I'm taking him to the health clinic to get checked out. I think he might have been drugged. Whoever did this to him had him bound in duct tape—hands, feet, and mouth. It was crazy. Adele, what the hell is going on? Are you in danger?"

Adele was about to answer but heard scuffling from the other end of the conversation followed by the sheriff demanding he be able to speak to Adele. Lucas sounded tired. His words were slightly slurred as if he had been drinking.

"Adele, where are you? What are you doing?"

A breeze pushed some tree limbs against the roof of Adele's car, making a noise uncomfortably similar to fingernails on a chalkboard. "I'm fine, Lucas. You go to the clinic with Roland. I'll call you first thing in the morning."

The sheriff's slurred demand for answers was repeated. "Where are you?"

"I'm working," Adele replied. "Give the phone back to Roland."

This was followed by more sounds of scuffling. Adele could hear Lucas fighting with Roland to keep the phone. It was several seconds before Roland was again speaking. "Sorry about that. Uh, wherever you are, whatever it is you're doing, do you need any help?"

Adele's initial instinct was to simply say no, but then she reminded herself that she was all alone on top of a mountain in the middle of the night, waiting for someone to retrieve a bag of illegal drugs she had left after having been instructed to do so by the same person likely responsible for incapacitating the sheriff.

Be brave, Adele, but don't be stupid.

"I'm on Orcas Island—near the watchtower. Roland, I have a quick question for you. Remember you told me about when Bryce Workman showed up at your bank one morning angry about you having sold his mortgage to another lender?"

There was a pause. Adele knew Roland was likely confused by the sudden transition. "What?"

"I need you to think, Roland. It's very important. When Mr. Workman arrived, was there anyone else at your office that morning as well?"

It sounded as if Roland was switching the phone from one ear to the other. "Uh, yeah, actually there was. Why?"

"I need to know who it was, Roland. I need to know now."

Roland's confusion intensified. "What's going on, Adele? Is this related to what happened to the sheriff? Are you in danger?"

"Please, just tell me who else was there."

Roland cleared his throat. "It was Sergei. He was there. I need to know what all of this is about. I deserve to know. Is Sergei after you?"

"I'm fine. I'll call you in the morning. Just focus on Lucas right now. Goodbye." Adele ended the call and double-checked to make certain the phone's ringtone had been shut off.

With silence having been restored, the wait continued.

"You've come a long way since your first adventure on these islands, young lady."

Delroy Hicks sat in the MINI's passenger seat, the brim of his always-present fedora tilted over his twinkling eyes. He crossed one bony leg over the other and chuckled. Adele didn't question how it could be that a man who had died more than two years ago was sitting in her car, reminiscing about the past. She was simply glad to hear the former university professor's deep, Irish-accented voice, smell his pipe tobacco, and look upon his haggard, smiling face.

"Yes, indeed. You are in the thick of it now, aren't you?" he continued. *"Say, do you recall how that poor, wretched former sheriff reacted to the threat of having his troubled child taken from him."*

Adele remembered the moment all too well. She was the cause of its unfolding. It was the culmination of her first visit to the San Juan Islands, a trip initially motivated by an interview for her college newspaper with the reclusive author, Decklan Stone. Since it happened, despite her attempts to forget, Adele had found herself recalling the sound of gunfire—two shots in quick succession. One ended the life of a son. The other was self-inflicted and did the same for a father who could no longer live with the lie he had perpetrated for so long.

"Ah, memory can be such a burden, one that haunts us all to the very end. I wonder, though, was it love that pulled the trigger on that day

or merely guilt and shame over having been caught? It's a strange and powerful thing, is it not? That bond between parent and child. How far is a mother or father willing to go to keep a child from harm? Or to try and convince themselves they are doing everything possible to do so? Should such a parent be condemned outright, or do we attempt to better understand that motivation? How far would you be willing to go, Adele, to keep those you love most alive and well? Would you steal? Would you lie? Would you kill?"

Adele woke from her dream with a start, looked at the passenger seat, and found it empty. Outside, the earlier breeze had developed into a steady wind. It was twenty minutes until midnight. The MINI had been idling for nearly four hours. Adele checked to see how much fuel remained. The gauge indicated a quarter-tank. It was still more than enough to return to the ferry terminal and get back to Friday Harbor.

As long as I'm not stuck here until morning with the car still running.

The sound of Delroy's voice remained fresh in Adele's mind. She knew his words were a reflection of her own thoughts on who would be coming up the mountain to retrieve the bag left at the watchtower.

With Delroy's contemplations whispering to her, Adele's eyes began to once again close. She shook her head, shut off the heater, and rolled down both front windows. A blast of cold air rushed into the car's interior, momentarily pushing back Adele's fatigue and returning her focus.

Crap. What if someone came down the road while I was asleep? Adele rested her forehead against the steering wheel as she considered that disappointing possibility. *I'm a pretty light sleeper. I can't see me not waking up to the sound of a vehicle driving by. Then again, I've been running around off all day. I'm tired. It could happen.*

Adele looked up and stared out through the windshield. The road remained empty. The only sound was wind and stirring trees.

Should I check out the tower? See if someone was already there?

Midnight arrived. Adele remained, vacillating between going to the tower and staying put in her hiding place alongside the road. Her impatience finally won out. She had to know whether the bag was still where she left it. Adele reached down, put the car into gear, and then froze. Her eyes narrowed as she tried to confirm what she thought she saw.

The road was suddenly illuminated in light. Someone was coming. Adele could hear the whine of a small motor growing louder. She saw a single headlight, a dark blur, followed by the quick return of more darkness and silence.

A motorcycle?

It didn't fit the profile of the person Adele thought would be arriving to the tower. Again, she was gripped by indecision. Her eyes glanced at the clock.

12:10 a.m.

Just go!

The MINI lurched forward in a spray of dirt and gravel. Once she reached the paved road, Adele accelerated hard, determined to catch whoever was in the act of picking up the drugs. Only after she killed the headlights right before arriving at the tower did she fully consider the possibility that person could be armed and dangerous.

It's too late to turn back now. I just have to be careful.

Adele came to a stop at the very back of the parking lot, turned off the car, and got out. Moonlight streamed down through an opening in the cloud cover, coloring the area in white-tinged gloom. Adele could see the outline of the motorcycle parked just below the watchtower entrance. She advanced toward the tower as quietly as possible, looking up into the structure for any sign of where the other person might be. A helmet hung from the handlebars. Adele crept past the bike, stopped, and then turned around. She reached out, removed the key from the ignition, and put it into her pocket.

Adele moved inside and stood at the bottom of the stairs. No sound came from the tower's upper floors. She continued to wait, her ears straining to detect any indication of movement from above.

It was just a few more seconds until the shuffle of descending footsteps echoed down the stairwell. Adele retreated into a dark corner and pressed her back against the stones. The steps were quick, their source certain to arrive very soon.

Adele held her breath. She saw a shadow grow larger until it covered the wall on the opposite side of the room from where she stood. Someone emerged from the stairwell with the duffel bag slung over their shoulder. They wore black from head to toe: leather jacket, jeans, and a ski mask that covered their face. Adele watched from her hiding place as the person walked quickly outside and sat down on the motorcycle with the bag still hanging off their shoulder. Adele strained to get a better look at the stranger's reaction after discovering the key was missing.

The helmet was put back on and the backpack adjusted. The motorcycle driver looked down to stare at the empty ignition. Hands moved to frantically check pockets. Adele sensed the stranger's confusion. She took that moment to step forward. The helmet's visor was pushed up as the head of the person sitting atop the motorcycle slowly lifted. Each looked into the eyes of the other.

Adele dangled the missing key in front of her. "Looking for this?"

A gust of wind blew through the tower's open doorway. Tree limbs creaked overhead. The other's eyes glared back at Adele. They stepped off the motorcycle and stood, silent and waiting. Something about the person's posture bothered Adele. She glanced at the eyes, noted the width of the shoulders, the lack of height. It became clear that whoever had arrived to take the drugs wasn't who Adele thought they would be.

I was so certain.

"Who are you?"

The motorcycle driver's head tilted to the side. With one hand, they slid the bag off their shoulder while continuing to stare back at Adele. "You don't know me, but I know who you are. I've read your articles."

Adele's eyes widened.

It was the voice of a woman.

A woman with a gun.

25

"Give me the key and then back away." The woman kept the pistol pointed at Adele with one gloved hand while reaching out for the motorcycle key with the other.

"Are you working for Sergei?" Adele asked. "Is he the one who sent you?"

The gun inched closer to Adele's face. "I don't want to hurt you, little girl, but I will if you make me. I'm going to ask you just one last time. Give me the key."

Adele considered knocking the gun from the woman's hand. She was close enough. *But would I be fast enough?*

The risk was too great. Adele gave up the key.

"Now step back and stay put," the woman said. "Don't try and follow me."

The motorcycle was started. The woman put the duffel bag back over her shoulder, used the heels of her boots to push the bike backward several feet, and then turned the wheel sharply, riding away from the tower. Adele watched the bike move toward her car at the back of the parking area.

C'mon, don't do it.

The motorcycle came to a stop. A gunshot rang out. The bike took off. Adele waited a few seconds until the quickly fading whine of the motorcycle's engine signaled the woman was gone. She jogged to her MINI and confirmed what she already suspected would be revealed.

A tire had been shot out.

Adele shook her head, let out a frustrated sigh, and then set about removing the flat and installing the spare kept in the MINI's trunk. With the cold wind biting into the exposed skin of her hands and face, she worked in jaw-clenched silence. After nearly thirty minutes, the spare had replaced the bullet-damaged flat.

The first ferry from Orcas to Friday Harbor wasn't due to arrive until 6:40 a.m. That left more than five hours of waiting time. Adele considered the possibility the woman on the motorcycle would be waiting for the same ferry.

She could ditch the bike and take another vehicle. I'd never know. Or maybe she has a place here on Orcas.

Adele knew her chances of locating the woman, particularly in the short-term, were remote. She decided to return to Friday Harbor and discuss with Lucas what had happened at the watchtower. Then together, they could determine how they might proceed.

Nearly two hours later found Adele parked at the Orcas Island ferry terminal, once again waiting, watching, and trying not to fall asleep. She turned the car off to conserve gas. After a few minutes of changing positions in the driver's seat, trying to get comfortable, she gave up and turned on the radio. The Seattle station came in surprisingly clear. A song Adele didn't know had just concluded, replaced by one she instantly recognized. With a satisfied smile, she reached out, turned the volume up, and began to sing. The music transported her back to the previous day inside the little Roche Harbor church, watching Lucas Pine's own plaintive rendition of the same song as he prepared to join his father's remains with those of his mother.

Adele turned up the volume even more. Her eyes closed. Her head fell back. At first she whispered the lyrics but soon she was nearly shouting them. "Don't let us get sick. Don't let us get old. Don't let us get stupid, all right? Just make us be brave. And make us play nice. And let us be together tonight."

After the song ended, Adele shut off the radio and looked out the car's windows, feeling a bit embarrassed at having momentarily lost herself in the impromptu solo performance. The ferry terminal remained empty. Wind-swept waves rocked against the dock pillars, while the ominous wail of a nearby loon called out from the shore.

"Fortune smiles upon us, Ms. Plank. The Native American tribes of this region have long considered that song to be a harbinger of harmony and truth. Do you know the loon, unlike most other birds, has solid bones? It is what allows them to dive so far beneath the surface of the water and find the truth that hides below."

Those were words spoken to Adele by Delroy Hicks as they sat together under a hillside tree looking out over the idyllic waters of Deer Harbor. It was an early-morning stakeout during what had been Adele's first San Juan Islands mystery two summers ago. The loon's cry signaled that the emerging day's light was soon to follow.

Try as she might, Adele was unable to fight off her body's demand for rest. Though she couldn't recall when sleep took her, she knew the exact time that she was later awakened by the arriving ferry's horn blast.

6:43 a.m.

Adele looked around and saw a handful of other vehicles awaiting the ferry's arrival. None were motorcycles. Her phone rang. It was Lucas. Unlike the previous night, he sounded far more focused and alert.

"Are you still on Orcas?"

Adele rolled her head from side to side, attempting to work out the kinks of an uncomfortable sleep. "Yeah, the ferry is pulling up now. How are you doing?"

"I'm fine. Have a bit of a headache. The doctor who looked me over seems to think I was hit with a tranquilizer dart, the kind used on stray animals, nuisance dogs, that sort of thing. Whatever it was, it sure as hell knocked me out. I don't know if it was Sergei who actually did it, but I'm almost positive he's involved. It's the same problem as always with him—getting the evidence to prove it. Roland says you were at the watchtower last night and also asking him about Bryce Workman."

The ferry shifted into reverse as the captain adjusted the direction of its approach, compensating for the waves pushing against its portside. "I thought Workman might be involved in getting the drugs onto the islands. Now I'm not so sure. I found an entire bag full of unmarked pill bottles on Matia, stashed inside one of the bathrooms. It was put there by Sergei—he was the one driving that blue-hulled boat."

"*What?*" Lucas said. "Did you actually see Sergei make the drop?"

"I watched him go into the bathroom with a duffel bag and come back out empty-handed. Once he left, I went in and retrieved the bag myself and brought it back to Roche Harbor."

Lucas mumbled something to himself before asking his next question. "You still have the drugs?"

Adele paused. She knew Lucas was about to be angry with her. "No. That's why I was at the watchtower last night. After the funeral, I went looking for you. I found the shovel and your gun and then received a call from someone telling me they knew I'd taken the drugs and that if I wanted to see you alive again, I was to leave the bag inside the tower. So that's what I did."

"Dammit, Adele. Why didn't let me know about the drugs? And then you go to the watchtower all by yourself to give them back? You could have gotten yourself killed!"

The ferry's horn erupted again, announcing it had successfully docked at the terminal. "I believed I knew who would be showing up to retrieve the bag. I also knew you were in danger, and the person who called made it very clear I wasn't to tell anyone where I was going or what I was doing. Lucas, I did what I thought I had to do to keep you alive."

Lucas groaned. "You thought it would be Bryce Workman who came to get the drugs, but it wasn't."

A car drove around the MINI on its way to boarding the ferry. "No. It was a woman," Adele said. "I couldn't see her face, and I didn't recognize the voice. There was no accent. I don't think she was Russian."

"Why did you suspect Workman?"

"He was the one who first told you he saw the boat tied up at Matia. He lied about that. It was too dark, and his vision is too poor for him to have seen what he said he did. When I brought up the illegal drugs you suspected were coming into the islands, he took a particularly strong interest while also suggesting that something odd was going on with Bob Tinnis. I took the Tinnis information as a deflection by Workman in an attempt to throw me off his trail."

Two more cars drove around.

"I see," Lucas replied. "Well, you managed to lose a significant amount of evidence based upon a false assumption regarding a suspect. I can't wait to see what further mess you can make of an ongoing investigation as you continue to play detective. I know I asked for your help, your input, but what you did last night is a damn mess. Oh, and regarding the teenaged girl who overdosed there on Orcas, she snuck sleeping pills that had been legally prescribed to her mother. A check of her social media accounts showed she had been dealing with serious depression. At this point we suspect suicide. There is no link between the drugs taken by Carl Blime and the girl's death."

A truck honked its horn as it drove past Adele's. She could see the bearded face of its driver glaring at her. The MINI was the only vehicle left that had not yet boarded the ferry. "I'm sorry about losing the bag, Lucas. I didn't think I had a choice. I'll be back to Friday Harbor soon. We can talk more then. Will you be home or at the office?"

"It's going to take a lot more than some animal tranquilizer to keep me from doing my job. I'll be in the office by late morning. Let's sit down, compare notes, and see if we can find a way to nail that bastard Sergei."

Animal tranquilizer," Adele thought. *The voice that called me demanding I bring the bag to the watchtower was male. He's working with the woman on the motorcycle.*

"Lucas, where does Bryce Workman live? Here on Orcas?"

"Actually, he does. Why?"

A ferry worker stared at Adele with his arms held out at his sides, wondering if she was going to board. Adele pretended not to see him. "Where?"

Lucas sighed, sounding frustrated as much by his own confusion as he was over Adele's latest batch of questions. "He has a little cabin just outside Olga. I haven't been out that way in years. It's at the end of, uh, a dirt road called Woodvine or Woodwine—something like that."

Lucas's voice grew louder as he realized Adele's intent. "*Wait.* You get on that ferry, Adele. I want you back in Friday Harbor within the hour."

Adele started the car, turned the wheel, and put it into gear. "I have just a few more questions for him. I'll make the next ferry. I promise."

Lucas was yelling Adele's name as she ended the call. When he called again, she let it go to voicemail. When he texted her, she put the phone away and ignored the continued messages while driving the MINI back onto the main road and then speeding off toward Olga and the home of Bryce Workman.

With her confidence and clarity fully returned Adele was once again certain of what she would find.

26

Olga is an unincorporated collection of storefronts and residences that dot the rugged, dark-rock shores of Buck Bay just north of Obstruction Pass. The land trip from the ferry terminal to Olga requires a long drive along the island's Horseshoe Highway that leads directly through the center of the area's primary business hub, Eastsound. In the summer months, Eastsound is a somewhat smaller but nearly as busy version of Friday Harbor. In the winter months, that activity is diminished by more than half. Unlike Eastsound, which provides the commercial tax-base for Orcas, Olga is the island's artist-driven alternative, a proudly eclectic mix of young and old who often and ironically come to the enclave to be among others who, like them, want to be left alone.

Adele, feeling both tired and a little weak, decided she needed some coffee and food before continuing on to Bryce Workman's home. She saw a sign for a bakery café that advertised the best coffee on the island. She pulled off the road and parked in front of a narrow, single-story structure that appeared to have been converted from a home into a small restaurant. That was something those who paid attention could see often throughout the islands—a unique and highly motivated entrepreneurial spirit that was in stark contrast to the outwardly laid-back island vibe that, year after year, attracts so many tourists.

"Laid back" actually takes a lot of planning and work.

The early-morning air was cool but not uncomfortably so. The blue-pink sky promised the day would be filled with sun. Adele's entrance into the café was announced by the cheerful tone of a bell that hung over the door. She was immediately rewarded with the smells of rich coffee and fresh-baked pastries. There were only six square tables in the dining area, one of which was already occupied by an old man and his golden retriever. The man sat nearly still and totally silent, his only movement the slow rise of a coffee cup to his lips followed by an equally slow descent. The process was then repeated as the dog slept on the floor with his head between his paws near the man's feet.

"Good morning. I don't recognize you. Is this your first time at the Buck Bay Café?"

Adele looked at the dark-haired, ruddy-cheeked, middle-aged woman who greeted her and nodded. "It is."

The woman wiped her flour-covered hands against the white apron she wore and then extended one of those hands to shake Adele's. "Wonderful! We don't get as many first timers during the winter months. My name is Maria—Maria Poplowksi. Yes, it's Polish—no jokes! I've already heard them all. I do just about everything around here, from the cooking to the cleaning to patching the roof after a bad windstorm. That's the life of a sole proprietor, and I wouldn't have it any other way. After being fired from every other job I ever had, I figured it might be a good idea to work for someone who appreciates me for me. I couldn't find anyone, though, so I had no choice but to hire myself!"

Maria's laughter filled the room, which in turn caused the golden retriever to momentarily lift its head and look at the two women before quickly resuming its nap.

"Oh," Maria continued, "and the artwork you see on the walls. I did those, too. Yes, they are for sale, including the frames that another local artist makes for me. Okay, I see I'm talking a bit too much. You look a little overwhelmed. The thing is, I like to test everything I make in here, including the coffee. Well, after a few dozen tests, I'm on one heck of a caffeine kick. So if I get to talking too much, feel free to tell me to be quiet. I won't take offense."

"Be quiet."

The request came from the old man. Maria scowled at him and then smiled back at Adele. "That's Old Tom. He's my first customer every morning, rain or shine. It's been that way since I opened for business nine years ago. He lives two properties down from here. That's his idea of being funny."

Tom repeated his earlier request in exactly the same way. "Be quiet."

Maria rolled her eyes. "Such a funny, funny man you are, Tom. Now, don't go bothering my new customer. I want her coming back just as often as you do." She straightened her posture and motioned toward one of the window tables that overlooked the long wooden dock that extended out into Buck Bay. "Feel free to sit down over there. We offer some wonderful water views. During the summer months the boat traffic out there is really something to see. In the winter pretty much the only boat we have down there regularly is the local park ranger's. That's his tied up to the dock right now."

Adele walked over to the window and looked down at the narrow dock. She could clearly see the circular green San Juan County Parks Department emblem on the boat's aluminum hull. "That's Bryce Workman's boat?"

Maria nodded. "Uh-huh. His place is just a mile or so from here. If you see the boat tied up down there, it almost always means he's home. I'm pretty sure he spends more time on the water than he does dry land. You know Bryce?"

"A little," Adele replied. "I live at the Roche Harbor marina. We've spoken a few times. I'm Adele Plank."

Maria smiled. "Roche Harbor is such a nice place. I don't get over that way nearly as much as I should. What can I get you?"

Adele sat and her stomach growled. "I'll take a coffee, some cream, and then one of those fresh-baked pastries I smell coming from your kitchen back there."

Maria snapped her fingers. "I know just the thing. Be right back." She made good on her promise, returning with a cup of coffee and a large, buttery croissant. "Here you go, young lady. Now if you need anything else give me a shout and I'll be right on out."

Adele pointed toward the dock. "If you don't mind, I do have a question."

"Sure." Maria straightened her apron. "What it is it?"

"Have you ever seen a blue-hulled speed boat tie up to the dock down there?"

Maria's eyes widened. She glanced at Tom and then leaned down to whisper a reply. "Funny you should ask. I *did* see a boat like that down there about a week ago. It was a loud, obnoxious thing." She frowned. "And I saw something else, too. The man who was driving that boat, well, he was a mean-looking fella. I could hear him arguing with Bryce, who looked scared to death. Who talks to a park ranger like that? Yelling and pointing at him. I thought a fight was about to break out. I watched him get back on that horrible boat of his and tear out of the bay. I'm pretty sure Bryce's salary doesn't pay nearly enough to have to put up with that kind of treatment. That's the last kind of thing he needs to be dealing with, poor guy."

Adele took a bite of her croissant and washed it down with a sip of coffee. "You mean having to deal with his daughter's condition?"

Maria appeared surprised at the mention of Workman's daughter. "Oh, you know about that?"

Adele nodded. "Yes. Some of it. I know she's very sick."

"I just can't imagine how he's managed for as long as he has." Maria sat across from Adele. "And all those years, having to do it by himself. Well, at least he's getting some help now."

Adele's coffee cup paused inches from her mouth. "Help?"

From across the room the old man coughed loudly. "Be quiet, Maria."

"Oh, hush Tom! She already knows about Bryce's daughter. It isn't some state secret around here about the help he's been getting. And why should it be? I hope it works out for them."

Tom turned around in his chair to glare at Maria while jabbing a finger at Adele. "*She's* not from around here."

Maria's fleshy red cheeks reddened further. "Are you going to sit here in *my* place of business and tell me what I can and cannot say to my own customers?"

Tom grunted as he stood up and then let out a long, exasperated sigh. "If you bothered to pay better attention, you might have already figured out you're sharing that information with a reporter. She already told you her name—Adele Plank. You have her newspaper on your counter right over there."

Maria turned to look at the counter and then turned back to stare at Adele as Tom walked out the door shaking his head with his dog following close behind. "Oh, goodness, you *are* that reporter!"

"I am," Adele said. "Is that a problem?"

"Geez, I don't want everyone around here calling me a gossip." Maria got up looking annoyed. "Were you getting information from me for a story? Is that why you were asking me those questions?"

"I'm not here about a story. Not specifically, anyway. I certainly don't want to get you into any kind of trouble with your neighbors."

Maria's eyes darted to the left and right. She appeared to be struggling over how to react. "Bryce Workman is a good man, you understand? Among the people here in Olga, well, he's one of us. He always has been, and we stick together. We might drive into Eastsound for business, but we come back to Olga to live. That's all Tom was trying to remind me of. None of us want to see our private business splattered all over the pages of your newspaper. No offense."

Adele finished her coffee. "None taken."

"Can I get you a refill on that coffee?"

Adele shook her head. "I'm good. Thank you."

Maria's eyes narrowed as she cocked her head. From outside, Adele could hear the sound of a motor growing louder. "Huh," Maria declared. "It appears you have impeccable timing."

Adele was taking the last bite of her pastry when she looked up, even as Maria continued to speak. "That noise you hear is the person we were just talking about—the same one who is helping Bryce care for that poor little girl of his."

Adele felt her heart beating faster as she recognized the sound of an approaching motorcycle.

27

The bell above the café door rang, and a tall, lean-faced woman walked in. Maria greeted her with a wide smile and remarked she would have her to-go order ready soon. The woman nodded and sat down at the table nearest the door. Her auburn hair was cut short and streaked with gray. The skin of her face was weathered, and the corners of her mouth bookended by deep wrinkles. The woman's long-limbed body appeared to have held up to the passage of time far better than her face. The legs, encased in tight, dark jeans, were lean and strong. Her wide shoulders also hinted at a strength that would be considered uncommon for a woman. Despite it being winter, she wore a short-sleeve shirt, revealing thin, sinewy arms covered in multiple tattoos.

Adele continued to watch the motorcycle rider out of the corner of her eye and waited. Maria returned to the dining area holding a white bag. The old wood floors creaked as she moved toward the woman's table. "Here you go, Roxy. Tell Bryce hello for me, and Isabel, too."

The woman named Roxy left a five-dollar bill on the table, stood, and took the bag from Maria. She mumbled a thank-you and walked out. Adele had been listening carefully and was able to confirm Roxy's voice was the same voice from last night. She was the one who had picked up the bag of drugs left inside the watchtower and then shot out Adele's tire. She heard the motorcycle start and watched as it took off down the road away from the café.

Maria walked over to Adele and put her hands on her hips. "Why didn't you want me to introduce you two? You were asking all those questions about Bryce. You sure this isn't some kind of investigative report you're pulling on me? I might be all smiles on the job, young lady, but I'm no different from anyone else. I don't care to be lied to, especially when it might involve my friends and neighbors."

Adele got up, intending to be on her way to Bryce Workman's home where she was quite certain she would find Roxy's motorcycle parked outside. "I'm sorry I can't tell you much right now, Maria. I assure you that what I'm doing is trying to *help* your friends and neighbors, not hurt them. What brought me here isn't gossip and it isn't just some little newspaper story."

Maria looked Adele up and down as she bit down lightly on her lower lip. She nodded, seemingly satisfied by a just-arrived-at conclusion. "Okay."

"Before I go," Adele said, "would you care to tell me the connection Roxy has to Mr. Workman?"

A flash of doubt moved across Maria's eyes. Then the café owner's warm smile returned along with a quick shrug. "Well, it's like I told Old Tom. That information isn't any big secret. I don't see any harm in telling you about it. Roxy and Bryce share a child. Isabel is their daughter."

Adele promptly sat back down as she digested what Maria had just told her. She recalled Roland mentioning to her how Workman's wife had taken off several years ago, leaving him to raise a daughter by himself. "Isabel has multiple sclerosis, right?"

Maria dropped into the chair across from Adele and nodded. "She was diagnosed years ago. According to the doctors back then, she should have been dead by now. We hadn't seen Roxy around here for quite a while. It was a bit of a scandal when she left. Poor Bryce, he took it all pretty hard. I sure can't blame him for that. Then again, I feel for Roxy, too. She strikes most folks as a hard case, but I see the good in her."

With the café empty but for the two of them, Adele was pleased to find Maria far more willing to talk. "Did Roxy leave before or after finding out about her daughter's MS?

Maria frowned, seemingly offended by the question. "Of course it was before. When she left it didn't have anything to do with her daughter. It didn't even have anything to do with Bryce. He was a good husband to her. It was just, well, she sort of lost her head and ran off with someone else."

"Another man?"

Maria shook her head. "It was a woman. This big group of bikers rolled through here one summer and stayed for several weeks. Roxy ended up taking off with them. Well, more specifically, with *her*. It was one of those things nobody talked publicly about, but everyone knew. Isabel's diagnosis didn't happen until at least a year after Roxy left, and by then she was in prison down in Texas for trafficking illegal prescription drugs across the border. That's where she learned about her daughter's disease—in prison. Can you imagine? Knowing your little girl is dying and not being able to go see her? As soon as she was let out, Roxy was back up here. She doesn't look much like she did before she left. I don't mean the tattoos or the clothes. I'm talking about her eyes. That time in prison—it took something out of Roxy she knows she's never getting back. Breaks my heart to see what it's done to her. I really worry about what she might do to herself once Isabel is gone."

The bell over the door announced the arrival of another customer. Maria reached across the table and gave Adele's hand a quick squeeze. "Our little talk stays between us." She got up scowling. "Is Bryce in some kind of trouble?"

Adele looked out through the window at the park ranger's boat tied up to the Olga dock. A large seagull sat on the vessel's bow and appeared to be staring back at her. "I don't know for sure. I hope not."

Maria took a deep breath. "Okay, I'm trusting that you'll do right by that family, Roxy included. The last thing they need is more trouble. And don't be a stranger after this. Stop in again."

"I will. Thank you for the hospitality and the information." Adele stepped outside to a temperature that had noticeably warmed from the time she had arrived at the café. Only a few thin clouds passed overhead. The air was unusually still.

It only took a few minutes of driving around Olga for Adele to locate a sign labeled "Woodwine." She turned off the main road and began a slow drive down the single-lane dirt road that Lucas had told her would lead to Bryce Workman's home. Thick, tall brush bordered the road's left side, while a rusted-out barbed wire fence marked the right.

Adele was forced to come to a stop at a closed metal gate, upon which hung a red-and-black "No Trespassing" notice. She got out of the car and walked to the gate. She could see the top of a roof, indicating a home that was no more than a hundred yards beyond the gate. An assortment of pine trees that grew over the property made it impossible to see anything else.

The gate is unlocked.

There was a smooth groove in the hard-packed earth where the bottom of the gate rubbed as it was repeatedly opened and closed. Adele put her hands on the dull, weathered metal and prepared to push it open. At the very moment she began to lift and push, she heard the sound of brush moving directly behind her.

"You don't read so well, do you?"

It was Roxy. Her tone made clear she wasn't happy to have found Adele preparing to ignore the sign. "Don't turn around. Don't move. I have the same gun I was pointing at you last night. You really think I didn't notice your car parked at the café? You're way out of your depth, coming here. I'm the last person you want to get caught following."

Adele opened her mouth to plead her case, to let Roxy know she was just there to talk but she never had the chance.

28

Rubbing alcohol.

That was the smell assaulting Adele's senses as she opened her eyes and looked around. She was sitting in a chair with her hands bound tightly behind her. Her feet were tied together by rope as well.

It was a small space. A narrow bed sat against the wall to the left, which had a single window covered by a dark curtain. Next to it was a white, three-drawer dresser, on top of which stood a lamp with a Cinderella shade. A multicolored throw rug covered most of the wood floor.

It's a girl's room.

There was a closet with a sliding door to Adele's right, and next to that, a closed door. Adele shut her eyes as the back of her head and neck sent shots of pain coursing through her upper body. She blinked several times to make certain her vision wasn't blurred. Her eyesight remained clear and sharp.

Guess that means I probably don't have a concussion.

Two voices, one male and one female, were arguing somewhere beyond the door. The sound was muffled, making it difficult to hear what they were saying. Adele leaned forward in the chair, straining to make out the words.

"What were you thinking? You could have killed her! She's friends with the sheriff. He probably already knows she was on her way here. There's at least one witness at the café; anyone else might have seen her driving down the road. My god, Roxy, we're no good to Isabel if we're *both* in prison."

"That won't happen. I'm never going back there. Do you understand? *Never*."

Even through the walls of the home, Adele could feel the conviction that fueled Roxy's promise to never return to prison. She was a woman who feared death far less than life behind bars. It was a determination Adele had badly underestimated, as evidenced by the throbbing lump in the back of her head.

And that makes her very dangerous—a person capable of doing almost anything.

"Roxy, if the sheriff and his deputies show up here, it will go bad, and quick. There won't be a way out. You can die fighting. I can die, too. It doesn't matter. Whether we live or die, either way, we lose Isabel. They'll take her from here. They'll take her from *us*, and that means she'll die alone."

Adele flinched at the sound of a hard slap.

"Shut up! I won't let you talk like that, Bryce. Isabel can hear us. You know she understands. Don't say those things to me. Don't say them to her."

The floors vibrated with the heavy thump of quickly approaching footsteps. There was a pause. Adele watched the door and waited. Someone was breathing on the other side.

The handle turned. The door opened. Bryce Workman, wearing his park ranger uniform, walked into the room and closed the door behind him. His eyes avoided looking at Adele. His head hung low. He paced back and forth and then sat down on the bed with his hands covering his face. When Bryce spoke, his voice cracked. "I'm so sorry, Ms. Plank. Roxy, she's scared. Not for her but for our daughter. The walls are closing in on us, and Roxy wasn't thinking right. Hell, she hasn't been right since she got back. Every waking moment she's fighting to keep Isabel alive."

Bryce's hands fell from his face. He looked up. Strands of unwashed hair were plastered to his sweat-drenched forehead. He looked at her with red, swollen eyes that spoke of a desperation Adele knew suggested she might never leave Orcas Island alive. The park ranger sniffled as he wiped his nose with the back of his hand.

"Ms. Plank, please, I don't know what to do. I don't want to hurt you. I really don't. It's my daughter. My little girl. I'm just trying to keep her safe." Bryce dropped his gaze as his fingers dug into the wool blanket covering the bed. Adele remained silent, knowing the wrong words could make the likelihood of her own death inside that room go from possible to probable.

Bryce's head slowly lifted. Tears streaked his face as his lower lip trembled. "If she gets any more scared of this going wrong, Roxy won't let you leave here alive. Do you understand? She won't allow it. I need to know. Is the sheriff going to be coming for you? Please don't lie to me, Ms. Plank. Tell me how much trouble we're in."

Adele attempted to straighten in the chair as much as the ropes that bound her would allow. She saw the park ranger's weapon inside the holster that hung off his hip and wondered whether a bullet would soon be meant for her. When she opened her mouth to speak, another stab erupted from the back of her head. Adele closed her eyes, gritted her teeth, and forced herself to ignore the pain.

The timing of that pain was fortunate as it momentarily prevented Adele from speaking. Instead, her mind had a few more seconds to reconsider what should be said to a distraught Bryce Workman, a man who appeared on the verge of a complete breakdown. It was within that brief space of time that a plan was formed. Adele could hear the words. She could see it clearly. It would require a great deal of convincing, first Bryce and Roxy, followed soon after by Lucas. And finally, it would need Roland's willing participation.

Bryce sat at the edge of the bed listening intently to Adele as she explained the possibilities of what could be done to bring both Roxy and him back from the brink and allow them to continue caring for their daughter. Soon the strain on his face lessened, and a hint of hope returned to his eyes. When Adele finished, he sat looking at her without saying anything for some time. Adele could sense his lingering uncertainty.

He shook his head. "I want to believe it's possible. You really think the sheriff will listen to you? That he would be willing to do that for us?"

"I know he'll listen," Adele said. "And yes, I think in the end, he'll agree. He wouldn't be doing it for *you*, Mr. Workman. Lucas would be doing it for your daughter. There is no other acceptable alternative. I'm offering a way out. A way for you to help make right what you have allowed to go so wrong. Your job now is getting Roxy to buy in. The sheriff *is* coming, and when he does, she can't be taking any 'last stand' nonsense. That'll just get her killed and leave Isabel without her mother."

Bryce closed his eyes tight, looking every bit like someone who at that moment would give anything to have the power to go back and make far different choices than the ones that had brought him to a time and place where a young woman was tied up to a chair inside his home.

"I'm putting my future in your hands, Ms. Plank—my future, Roxy's future, and our daughter's."

Adele nodded. "I know. I don't intend to let any of you down."

Bryce stood, crossed the room, and proceeded to untie Adele. "I hope you don't. There's someone I want you to meet. I need to further explain how all of this happened. It won't excuse what I've done to you and the sheriff, but maybe you'll understand."

When Adele tried to stand her legs buckled. She feared she was going to be sick. Bryce reached out and held her up. "Take a few deep breaths," he whispered. "There, feel better now?"

Adele nodded. Though her legs remained weak, she was able to walk.

Bryce opened the door and guided her down a narrow, wood-floored hallway. The smell of rubbing alcohol grew even stronger. Adele noted the collection of photographs that hung from the hallway walls. Nearly all of them included images of a beautiful, happy little girl.

"These are all Isabel?"

Bryce stopped and nodded. He pointed to one of the larger-framed pictures. "That is one of my favorites."

The photograph showed a grinning, dark-haired girl seated behind the wheel of the same San Juan Islands Parks Department boat that Adele had seen tied up to the Olga dock. Behind Isabel was her father with both hands on his daughter's shoulders, his smile as wide as hers.

"That was one of the last times she ever went out on the boat with me. Within six months of that picture being taken she struggled to get out of bed. In a year she could barely talk. And after that? Well, you'll see."

As they entered the home's main living area, Adele could hear the soft hiss of an oxygen tank in use. Directly beside the room's large bay window was a hospital bed. The blinds were drawn back, revealing an expansive view of fields and trees and beyond, a glimpse of glistening, blue-green island waters. A short table stood at the foot of the bed, atop which sat sponges, bottles of rubbing alcohol, and stacks of books.

Isabel's mother sat in a chair next to the bed, holding her daughter's hand. Roxy turned and glared at Adele, her eyes blazing an all-too-clear warning she would do whatever necessary to keep Isabel from harm. Bryce's soft voice was a stark contrast to his wife's seething protective instinct.

"This is our Isabel," he said. "We recently celebrated her birthday, a birthday the doctors said would never come."

Adele moved from behind Bryce to look down on the teenage girl swathed in white sheets. She recognized the same dark hair from the photographs in the hallway. The hair was the only thing that looked the same, though. Isabel's badly swollen face, partially covered by an oxygen mask, was without expression, as if each individual muscle had been removed. The corners of her mouth hung down each side of her chin. The dull, half-open eyes drooped. It was a tragic mask, particularly on the face of one so young.

"The buildup of fluid causes the swelling." Bryce sighed. "It became a lot worse when she could no longer move on her own. We try and exercise her arms and legs as much as possible. That seems to help some. The rubbing alcohol is to prevent the bedsores from becoming infected. Sepsis is a constant concern."

"Have you considered putting her in a facility designed to care for patients like her?" Adele asked.

Roxy shook her head while gently stroking the top of Isabel's hand. "The nearest one is in Seattle, and that's where people like Isabel are sent to die. They don't treat the disease in those places. They just watch and wait for what they try to convince you is the inevitable. Besides, they would *never* love her like we do."

Bryce moved into the adjoining kitchen and then returned, holding a plastic pill bottle. "*These* are why we're doing all this. They're the only things we've found that helped to slow the disease. Normally, her form of multiple sclerosis would have killed Isabel years ago. These pills, they've kept her going. She can't swallow an entire pill anymore, so we grind them down and mix them with her water she takes from a straw. The problem is our insurance won't cover the cost of the medicine. The drug doesn't have FDA approval, and that approval likely won't come for another two or three years. She was first given them during a six-month trial with a handful of other MS patients. Within weeks, Isabel was doing better. She was stronger. When the trial ended, they took the drug away due to alleged complications with some of the other patients. When I followed up a few months later, I was told revisions had been made to the protocols to ensure FDA compliance but that Isabel would not be considered for the next trial. Her disease was deemed to have progressed too far."

Roxy angrily wiped away a tear. "The bastards were just going to let her die. They don't care. To them, Isabel is just a statistic."

Bryce then explained how he came to work for Sergei. "I spent weeks making calls, sending letters and emails to anyone and everyone on how I could obtain access to the drug. Each time I was told it was impossible. Without FDA approval, the drug remained illegal inside the United States. In the meantime, Isabel's condition continued to worsen. So, I looked outside the country and eventually found someone willing to provide it to me illegally—for a price. Almost every penny I made went toward purchasing the medicine. When that wasn't enough, I sold most of my belongings, cashed out my retirement, and then refinanced my home, which, of course, I couldn't afford to pay back. I didn't care. All I could think about was trying to keep Isabel alive. What if they found a cure, some new treatment, this year or the next? I can't allow her to just fade away from us without fighting with her as hard as she's still fighting. She wants to live. Without any doubt, I know that to be true."

"And that's how you came to know of Sergei Kozlov," Adele said. "It was the morning you went into the bank to complain about your mortgage having been sold to another lender."

Bryce grimaced as he nodded. He didn't bother asking Adele how she had already come to have that information. "That's right. He overheard me yelling at Mr. Soros. I was scared, stupid, and said too much. A man like Sergei, that just smells like opportunity. We struck a deal. I relayed to him as much as I knew about the sheriff's schedule and border patrols—any information I might have that would help him to safely transport the drugs to the islands. In return, he paid me cash to help cover the cost of Isabel's medicine. When I had second thoughts, Roxy convinced me to keep going. Yes, it was a deal with the devil, but that devil was helping to keep our little girl alive when no one else would."

"But you *did* try to find a way out, didn't you?" Adele said. "When you told the sheriff you saw the boat at Matia. You wanted Sergei to get caught."

With narrowed eyes, Roxy's head snapped to the side to look up at her husband, a reaction that made it clear she hadn't known what Bryce had tried to do.

"We've managed to stockpile some of Isabel's medication," Bryce replied. "It's enough to get by for several more months. I learned the sheriff was dealing with an unusually high amount of drug-related service calls lately, and it wasn't hard to make the link between that and my helping to bring those pills into the islands. When I was told about Carl Blime's death and then later learned of the young girl here on Orcas who was hardly older than Isabel, I couldn't take it anymore. Something had to change. Yes, I was hoping Sheriff Pine would catch Sergei and I would no longer have to be involved in his drug-trafficking scheme."

Adele suddenly remembered what Lucas had told her about the girl's death. "The drugs that killed the girl were from taken from her mother. They were prescribed. The sheriff thinks it was a suicide. Her death wasn't related to the drugs Sergei was bringing in."

Roxy got up. For the first time, Adele sensed the more sensitive woman that yet remained somewhere deep within her prison-hardened exterior. "Really? He told you that?"

Adele nodded. "Yes, earlier this morning."

Bryce ran a hand down the front of his face. "Thank god I had nothing to do with that poor girl's death." He looked at Adele with eyes once again wet with emerging tears. "Thank you for telling me that. You have no idea how the news of that tragedy has haunted me since I was first told of it."

An arm rested around Adele's shoulders. It was Roxy. The hard edge in her voice had softened considerably. "Let me introduce you to our Isabel."

Adele sat in the chair next to the bed. Roxy placed her hands on Adele's shoulders. "She can hear you. We put the bed here because it's the only place in the house where you can see a little bit of the water. Isabel loves being on the water, don't you honey? I used to joke how she had a fishing pole in her hands before she could walk. She and Bryce would come back with one of those big old ugly Ling Cod, slap it down on the picnic table outside, and we'd fillet it together. She was no older than five or six and demanding I let her do it all by herself. Her little hands would be mixing the batter up in the bowl, and then we'd drop all that tasty fish into the deep fryer. Those really were the best of times for us."

"Until you took off." Bryce's words cut as sharply as a fillet knife. Roxy's cheeks turned crimson. She glared at her husband but then just as quickly, her anger dissipated. Adele sensed the mother's terrible guilt over having left her child and the even greater fear that it would be her child who might soon be leaving her.

Roxy squeezed Adele's shoulders. "Go on. Let her know who you are."

Adele was surprised to find herself feeling so nervous and then equally surprised to see her hand reach out to take hold of Isabel's. The skin was especially soft and cool to the touch. "Hello, Isabel. My name is Adele. I'm very happy to meet you."

This introduction was followed by a brief moment of awkward silence. Adele followed Isabel's gaze to the window and the world outside. From the chair, she was able to see what Isabel saw, including the blue-green glimmer of the sea.

"I learned how to drive a boat by myself recently," Adele said. "I had a friend who showed me. I'm just like you. I love to get out on that water and feel the wind in my face and hear the waves hit the hull as we pass over them. My friend died, but there are moments when it's like he really is still here. He even talks to me sometimes. That probably sounds weird, but it's true. He was a professor and had this wonderful, deep Irish voice. And he was always trying to have a good time. Even when he was sick, he *always* made time to laugh. I'm pretty sure there's a lesson we can all take from that. His name was Delroy Hicks. He knew another friend of mine who was the reason for my coming to the islands in the first place. His name is Decklan Stone. He's a writer."

Adele felt one of Isabel's fingers twitch. She looked over just in time to see the girl's eyes blink twice.

Bryce stepped forward and stood directly next to the Adele. "She knows all about Decklan Stone. We have his book on the table at the end of the bed. I've read it to her at least a dozen times over the last year alone. Isn't that right, Isabel?"

This time two of Isabel's fingers moved. To most able-bodied people it would have been an insignificant gesture, but for Isabel such a thing had become a rare moment of life, one that caused both her parents to smile. Bryce reached over and grabbed the torn and tattered hardcover edition of Decklan Stone's *Manitoba* from the table. Adele looked up at him.

"You mind?" Bryce asked. He handed her the very same story that Adele, like Isabel, had grown up loving to read. Like all great novels, that book became a bond between others who had read it as well, a shared experience and understanding that extended beyond the limiting borders of individual lives.

Adele opened the cover and lightly ran her fingers across the yellowed pages. She looked down and once again heard Decklan's words that first spoke to her years ago from across the chasm of time gone and experience gained. Adele glanced up at Isabel, smiled, and recited the book's introduction, which she knew by memory, out loud.

"My hatred did not come naturally to me. I wasn't born into such a state. Rather, it was taught to me by all those who doubted and by all those who pretended to care. So there it was—the hate that divided became our greatest bond—the thing we knew best and certainly far more than we knew ourselves. Hate had become my single greatest love, the only thing I could count on to never disappoint me as all the others inevitably would. I breathed its air. I wore its clothes. And when I looked into the mirror, it was hate happily staring back. And that was okay. That was fine. That was my life, such as it was. We were all alone together, those too many voices, the collective din, screaming in silence. Then came that unexpected trip to the place where it truly is darkest before the light. A journey of revelation and revolution from which everything I thought had been, never was, never could be, and never would be again—Manitoba."

Roxy used a cloth to wipe away the tears that tracked down her daughter's cheeks. "See? She's as aware inside of her own head as any of us are."

This time it was Adele who squeezed Isabel's hand. Together they both looked through the window and watched in silence the world outside. When the hard knock Adele knew would come finally did, and the sheriff's voice rang out, demanding the door be opened, Adele stood and looked at Bryce and Roxy.

"This is where I need you both to trust me." Adele's eyes lingered on Roxy, waiting for acknowledgement.

Roxy nodded. "I trust you. I just hope we can trust him." She tilted her head toward the door beyond which Lucas stood waiting for it to be opened.

He called out again. "Bryce, open the door. If you don't, I *will* break it down. I know your daughter is in there. I don't want to scare her, so you need to open up now."

Adele walked to the door. She would be the one to open it. "Lucas, it's me. I'm okay and I'm coming out. We need to talk. Are you alone?" There was a pause. Adele imagined Lucas rolling his eyes, wondering how Adele had managed to become the spokesperson for the Workman home.

"I have Deputy Smith out here with me," Lucas replied. "She's watching the road."

"You don't need her here. In fact, I think it would be best she doesn't hear what I'm going to ask of you. The fewer people know, the better."

Lucas let out a long sigh. "What are you up to *now*, Adele?"

"Just give me a chance to explain—alone. If I can't convince you, well, you're going to do what you think you need to anyway."

There was a frustrated groan from the other side of the door followed by several seconds of silence. "I tell you what. You come out here so I can confirm you are in fact okay and I'll tell Chancee to wait for me back at the gate. Otherwise, you need to step away because I will be kicking this door in."

Adele turned back and gave Bryce, Roxy, and Isabel a reassuring smile. "It's going to be fine. He'll listen." Right before she went to pull the door open Bryce coughed.

"Please let the sheriff know I'm awful sorry for shooting him with that tranquilizer dart," he said. "When the bag went missing, Sergei was convinced it was you or the sheriff, or both of you, who took it. The fact is, Sergei was scared, which made me even more scared. It meant the ones he answers to likely gave him an ultimatum, and I'm pretty sure those people are capable of anything. He threatened to show up here and look for the bag himself, and if he didn't find it, well, I didn't want it to come to that. I had to try and get that bag back myself."

Again, Adele reached for the door, and again she was interrupted. This time it was Roxy. "And I'm sorry for hitting you on the back of the head like I did. When I realized it was you following me, I just reacted."

"It's going to be fine," Adele said. She wasn't sure of that, but she was going to do her best to make it so.

Adele opened the door.

29

Lucas had his weapon drawn and ready to fire as Adele stepped outside. He tilted his head trying to look past Adele into the home.

"See?" Adele said. "I'm fine. You can put that down."

Lucas's eyes narrowed. "What did they do to you?"

Adele motioned for him to follow her as she took a few steps away from the front door. "I said I'm fine. I just came here to speak with them. They're inside with Isabel."

Lucas frowned. "There's someone else besides Bryce in there with his daughter?"

Adele quickly explained about Roxy's return from her time in prison. Lucas wasn't aware she was back. He holstered his gun and shrugged. "Okay, now then tell me what's going on here. What do you need to talk to me about?"

Adele spent the next few minutes detailing what motivated Bryce and Roxy Workman to do what they did as well as her idea on how to push Sergei's Russian associates out of the islands for good. Lucas listened intently without saying a word, allowing Adele to finish without interruption. When she looked up at him for a reaction, he shook his head.

"I can't let slide what Bryce did to me. I already knew it was him because besides the people at the chapel, he was the only one I told where I would be following the service. The county parks department oversees the Roche Harbor Cemetery. I needed his approval to place my father's remains at my mother's grave. He knew exactly where I would be and when. Now you want me to give him a pass for shooting me with a damn animal dart? That's not how this job works, Adele. He assaulted an officer of the law. He left me unconscious and tied up at the mausoleum. You just explained how it was him who has been helping Sergei get those drugs into the islands. There is no way in hell I look the other way on any of that. I understand his daughter is very sick, but the law is the law. It's what I'm sworn to uphold. It's the only thing that keeps the rest of us safe from people like Sergei. I'm sorry. I have no choice but to go into that house and arrest Bryce."

When Lucas took a step toward the front door, Adele placed her hand on his chest and pushed back. "No."

"Get out of my way."

Adele stood her ground. "You're not listening. Doing the right thing isn't going in there and arresting Bryce Workman in front of his daughter. It's just you being an ass."

Lucas looked down at the hand that remained pushing against his chest. "I'll arrest you, too. Don't think I won't. This is my job. You *know* that. And if I don't do my job, I'm no better than Bryce Workman."

"You said your job is keeping the people of these islands safe. If you want to do that you need to go after Sergei and the people he's working for. Use Bryce to help you with that. He wants to help. He wants to be a part of fixing this mess. If you arrest Bryce, Sergei will just find someone else, and you'll be right back where you started. You'll be reacting to trouble instead of getting out in front of it. Give my way a chance."

Adele detected a hint of consideration in Lucas's eyes that informed her he was finally listening. He took a step back and turned around with his hands on his hips. High above their heads a bald eagle circled slowly before suddenly descending and coming to rest on a tree branch where it cocked its head, observing them. The great bird of prey appeared to be anticipating what the sheriff's next response would be as much as Adele was.

Lucas turned around and ran a hand through his short-cropped hair. "You really think you can convince Roland to go along with your plan? He's sunk a hell of a lot of money into that project. Roland Soros has always been about taking things, not giving them away."

"I like my chances," Adele replied. "I can be pretty convincing when I want to be."

Lucas chuckled. "Yeah, I can't argue that." He kicked the dirt with the toe of his boot and then nodded. "Okay. If you can get Roland to agree, I'll try it your way. We won't catch Sergei quickly, you know. And that's if we actually catch him at all. He'll be extra cautious for a while, hanging low. Though if Roland goes along with this, Sergei won't be too popular with the people he answers to, including Yuri Popov."

"That's a big reason why I think this will work. Sergei will be isolated, weak, and much more likely to make a mistake, and when he does you'll be there waiting. And remember, he's not doing this alone. Bryce was giving Sergei information on the safest times and routes into the islands. He wasn't actually the one picking up the drugs from Matia. Someone else was helping Sergei with that—someone on the islands. We isolate Sergei, we isolate that other person as well. You could have a chance to take them *all* down. It'll just take more time."

Lucas arched a brow. "Ms. Plank, I do believe you have all the makings of a criminal mastermind—or a politician."

Adele smiled. "Aren't they both pretty much the same thing?"

Lucas shrugged "Yeah, I suppose they are." He paused and then tipped his head toward the house. "How's their daughter Isabel doing?"

"Why don't you come inside and see for yourself."

Adele led Lucas back to the front door. She saw the apprehension on his face. It was the look of uncomfortable uncertainty so common to those confronted by the sight of someone they knew was near death. he had seen enough of sickness in recent months.

They walked into the home. Bryce and Roxy got up from their place next to Isabel's bed. Roxy's mouth was a tight slash across her deeply lined face, a mother bear ready to defend her cub. Bryce was more hopeful. He had already removed his gun and set it on the kitchen counter several feet behind him to help reassure the sheriff he meant him no further harm. He also held the same duffel bag Adele had taken from Matia and then left at the watchtower. He handed the bag to the sheriff with yet another apology as he did so. Lucas opened it, confirmed its contents, and then gave both Bryce and Roxy a grateful nod. He went on to explain to the couple his willingness to go along with Adele's plan in the hope of getting rid of Sergei once and for all. Lucas also made clear to Bryce there would be no second chances.

"I get even a whiff of you doing something wrong, I'll have no choice but to take you down for good, Bryce. You never should have allowed yourself to be used by Sergei like this."

Roxy stepped toward Lucas, her penetrating, gunmetal eyes answering the sheriff's warning. "I know you're right about that. I also know it's a hell of a lot easier to judge us for what we did than it is to live with the reasons for why we did it. I heard about your father dying and I'm sorry for your loss. Ask yourself what you would have been willing to do to turn back the disease that took your dad's mind from him. To make him healthy and whole again. Really think about it, Sheriff. And after you're done thinking, take another moment to remind yourself that we're not talking about an old man who lived a long, full life. It's our daughter. Our little girl. Look at her. Look at her lying in that bed. Look at her and tell me you can't conceive of parents who find themselves willing to take such a terrible risk."

Roxy moved aside and pointed to Isabel. "Go on, Sheriff. *Look at her.*"

Minutes later, after returning outside, Adele watched Lucas walk quickly from the home and then stop with his back to her. He held the duffel bag under his arm. In the tree directly above him, the eagle remained, looking down at them. Heavy clouds were making a slow return to the island skies, accompanied by a drop in temperature.

Lucas turned around. His face was grim, his eyes seething. Adele knew the brief time spent with Isabel had affected him greatly. "We need to get that son of a bitch. People like Sergei have no business being on these islands. We can't allow filth like him in." He shook his head. "No, we kick their ass out. The family in that home didn't deserve to be poisoned by the likes of Sergei Kozlov and the people he works for. Mark my words Adele. I *will* get him."

"I know, Lucas. We just need to be patient. It'll happen."

The eagle suddenly spread its massive wings and with a soft whoosh of air, flew off toward the approaching clouds.

"First, you need to get Roland to agree," Lucas said. "If you don't succeed in doing so, I won't have time to be patient. And I sure as hell won't be sitting back, letting more of those drugs come into the islands." He turned and began making his way back to the gate where Deputy Smith awaited his return.

Adele called out after him. "What will you do if I can't convince Roland?"

Lucas stopped again. Adele couldn't see his face, but his voice hinted of something dangerous. He was a slowly simmering pot that now threatened to boil over. "I'm starting to understand how doing what *should* be done isn't always what the law says *must* be done. I've come to learn that sometimes the law has nothing to do with what's really right or wrong. I also know that if I go after Sergei directly, it won't be the law that finds him. It'll be me. God help him when I do. Good luck with Roland. Let me know how it goes."

After Lucas left Adele looked down at her phone. It was late afternoon and time to return by ferry to Friday Harbor. Once there she would meet with Roland to convince him to agree to her plan. It was at that moment he might possibly hold the fate of the islands between two very different choices.

What will you choose, Roland? Will it be yes, or will it be no?

30

Adele watched Roland as he looked out at the vast, white-capped waters of the Strait of Juan de Fuca. The worsening wind didn't seem to bother him. He stood with his hands stuffed into the pockets of his jacket and his legs spread shoulder-width apart, smiling silently to himself as he appeared to ponder the proposal Adele had spent the last ten minutes explaining to him. She had made her pitch. Now she waited for a response.

Initially, Adele had intended to meet with Roland at his home but then changed the location to the Cattle Point project since it was that project that was so critical to her plan to end his dealings with the Russians and the Russian's dealings with the islands.

They stood next to a ten-foot-high "Coming Soon" sign depicting the massive hotel and entertainment complex Roland had long hoped to bring to the area. Behind the sign were wide swaths of earth that had already been moved in preparation for the pouring of the foundation. The project was to have been Roland's way of finally outgrowing the long shadow of his grandfather who had been such an influential businessman in the region's economic and political development during the latter half of the twentieth century.

Adele knew what she asked of Roland was no small thing. She was also equally convinced it was the right thing both for Roland and the people of the San Juan Islands.

Roland turned to look at Adele. The grin was no longer there. His face was without expression, unreadable, leaving Adele to worry her idea was about to be denied. He turned all the way around to face her, his hands still stuffed into his pockets. The wind struck his face fully, causing his hair to push back against his scalp. His eyes lingered on Adele for some time before his gaze broke away from her to look skyward.

Those eyes eventually lowered again, slowly and deliberately. Roland cocked his head to the side, smiled at Adele, and then winked. "Sure, why not? Let's do it your way. You're right, of course. I remember when I was a boy coming back from fishing or crabbing, my grandmother would always remind me to not leave any of the fish guts or crab shells in the backyard because it would go bad and attract rodents."

He looked up at the "Coming Soon" sign. "This thing I tried to create, it *has* gone bad. I see that now. It's all gone bad, and it's attracting the rats. Yuri Popov is one big, fat, dangerous rat, and I'm responsible for bringing him here. Where I see jobs, opportunity, and an expanded tax base, he sees thousands of tourists from all over the world to whom he can sell his drugs, his women, his men, illegal gambling, and whatever else a man like that deals in. I thought I could control him—keep him at arm's length until I paid him back what I owed. He didn't want to just get paid back, though. He wanted it all. He wanted to break me so that I had no choice but to hand this over to him after it was finished."

Roland's jaw clenched. "And then he burned down my boat. Okay, he burned me, so let's burn him. Let's burn Popov, and Sergei, and the whole lot of them who thought they could come here and take what I understand now was never mine to give—these islands, this place, our home."

"Can you raise enough cash to actually buy Yuri out?"

"I can do it," Roland answered. "I'm going to have to leverage some serious debt on every one of my properties. It will push the boundaries of normal banking practice, which I've managed to avoid to this point, but what the hell, right? It isn't living if it isn't living dangerous from time to time. I hold the title to Cattle Point outright. Yuri has no legal claim. He wouldn't want to. That would require an investigation into his own business dealings by county and state officials which of course he would never allow. He won't be happy but once I change what I intend to do with Cattle Point, Yuri will lose all interest in it. He'll get his money back and be on his way."

Roland scratched the stubble on his cheek and arched a brow as the familiar grin returned. "It's a good plan. It also happens to be the right thing to do."

Adele returned the smile. "I didn't think you'd be so easy to convince."

"A few days ago, I wouldn't have been." Roland looked around at the project site and sighed. "You helped to give me perspective. I got so caught up in thinking this property was going to define me I became willing to do almost anything to make it happen. If my grandfather were here, he'd be explaining how that mindset leads to bad business. When ego gets in the way of common sense, that's a business in trouble. I guess that means you better stick around so you can keep me out of trouble, huh?"

Adele stepped forward and gave Roland a hug as the wind whipped around the both of them. When she attempted to end the embrace, Roland held her tight. She felt his finger caress the bottom of her chin and lift her face upward to meet his. *Am I the real reason he agreed to end the Cattle Point project?* She turned her face and pushed away from him.

"I have to know you're doing this because you want to, Roland. Because you really do think it's the right thing. Your decision can't have anything to do with me or what happened between us."

Roland's hands returned into his pockets. He attempted another smile, but it didn't entirely hide his disappointment. "You have nothing to worry about in that regard. What I do with this property has nothing to do with my feelings for you." He glanced down and issued a nervous cough. "I take it you haven't told Lucas about what happened on the yacht?"

Adele's eyes narrowed. "No. It's like you just said. My being here has nothing to do with that. Why? Are you going to tell him?"

Roland shook his head. "What happened that day was between you and me. I've never been a kiss-and-tell kind of guy. If Lucas finds out, that'll be up to you."

"I appreciate that."

Roland turned back around to face the sea. He pointed toward a gap in the cloud cover where the last of the late-day sun illuminated the snow-covered peaks of the Olympic Mountains. He held out his hand and motioned for Adele to join him. "Looks like it's going to be an amazing sunset. You want to watch it with me?"

Adele hesitated. She could see the corners of Roland's cheeks lift. He was smiling again. "Don't leave me hanging," he said. "Get over here."

She reached out and allowed Roland to take her hand into his. The clouds parted further, sending out golden slivers that appeared to bounce across the water and onto the San Juan shores. Even the wind seemed content to pause out of respect for the beautiful portrait Mother Nature was providing.

Roland squeezed Adele's hand. "It really is something, isn't it? I've travelled to a lot of places in this world but can't imagine choosing to live anywhere else but here. Thanks for taking the time to share this with me. Usually, I'm standing out here all alone."

Adele didn't say anything. There was no need.

Tomorrow would soon arrive, and along with it another article for the paper.

She had some writing to do.

31

The Island Gazette
Local Businessman Offers Hope Following Murder on Matia
by Adele Plank

The world has a prescription drug problem and America is by far its greatest addict. This addiction ends more American lives each year than auto accidents. And while fatal auto accidents continue to decline, prescription drug overdoses in this country have more than doubled in the last decade alone. Fifty of us now die each and every day from these manufactured drugs. These casualties are far more than mere statistics, though. They have names. They were real people with real experiences, relationships, dreams, and aspirations that have tragically gone silent. They were our mothers, fathers, sisters, brothers, sons, and daughters.

Lives cut short by the incessant need for a pill.

The San Juan Islands, this beautiful isolation we so happily call our home, is now under attack by those who would not help to solve the blight of addiction but rather seek to worsen it for profit. These are outsiders to our shores. People who lack the basic humanity to fully consider the trauma their greed inflicts upon others.

Longtime island resident Carl Blime was a recent victim of this poisonous endeavor. His lifeless body was found on the shores of Matia, marking that quaint and charming little island as a murder scene. The pills he took that ended his life were not legally prescribed. His addiction won out as addiction so often does, pushing him to take even greater risk, a hopeless cycle against which he fought alone and in silence. And that is how Carl Blime died—alone. It didn't have to be that way. We cannot allow our indifference to make us all accomplices to his murder. Carl didn't require our judgment or condemnation of his struggle. What he needed was our help.

Mr. Blime is not the only local casualty to this now-threatening epidemic. Sheriff Lucas Pine believes there have been others and that there will be more if we don't move quickly and decisively as a community to stop it. It is with that shared purpose in mind that local businessman Roland Soros has been motivated to make a remarkable contribution to the people of the San Juan Islands. He has donated the entirety of his Cattle Point property to the county with the strict stipulation that the land then be used as the location for a new addiction treatment facility. Island residents will be granted priority service. Mr. Soros has indicated construction can begin immediately and that the doors could open as early as next year. I urge all readers to contact members of the county council to make certain the completion of this project is expedited.

The need is great, and the time is now.

Let's all work together to make this happen.

———

Lucas stood directly underneath the new sign Roland had recently placed on the Cattle Point property:

Coming Soon: The Dr. Edmund Pine Addiction Rehabilitation Center at Cattle Point.

He held up the newspaper in his hand. "It's good, Adele—*real* good. You've managed to push Yuri Popov out of here without having to fire a shot. I still can't believe Roland was willing to give up the project. All that cash he sunk into it. I would have loved to have been a fly on the wall when Yuri received word of Roland's donation to the county. Talk about pulling the rug out from underneath someone."

Lucas looked up at the sign. Adele could see his eyes moving slowly from side to side as he read and reread the dedication to his father. The dedication was something Roland had come up with entirely on his own, a gesture as dignified and selfless as the man the rehabilitation center was to be named in honor of.

"He's a tough one to figure out, isn't he?" Lucas said. "Just when you think you have him nailed down, he does something like this that is so out of character with who you thought he was."

Adele knew exactly what Lucas meant. It's what made her own feelings toward Roland so complicated and conflicted. "Yeah, he can surprise you." Lucas's eyes lingered on her. She sensed he possibly heard something more in her words about Roland than he cared to. She moved quickly to change the subject. "Any news on Sergei?"

A faint, tight-lipped almost-grin flittered across Lucas's face. Adele's attempt to move the discussion away from Roland appeared to have only increased his curiosity over why she would try and do so. He looked away and shrugged.

"He'll most likely lay low for a while. I'm pretty certain his biggest problem right now is answering to Popov for losing Cattle Point. If Sergei survives Popov's disappointment, he'll be back here sooner or later."

Lucas went quiet. He pretended to be looking out at something on the water but Adele knew better. He was wondering about what might be going on between her and Roland. She prepared to finally tell him about the time on Roland's yacht. Her mouth opened then abruptly closed as she suddenly lost the courage to do so.

"Did you want to say something?"

Adele zipped up the front of her jacket and shook her head. "No. It's getting cold again." *Great,* she thought. *It's come to this. I'm talking about the weather.* She hated herself for not coming clean. Lucas deserved better. *Maybe he deserves better than me.*

"Spring is coming." Lucas breathed deep. "I can smell it. My mother's crocus flowers are just starting to bloom back at the house. She always said that was the first true sign the season was changing. Usually right around early April there would be at least one argument between Dad and her over the flowers or some plant. He was always trying to cut them back, and she was always telling him to leave them alone. One time he came marching into the house with a tear in his slacks, demanding justice against one of Mom's rosebushes. He said he was going out to the shed to retrieve the cutters. She met him in the backyard and ordered him to put them back. He stood there fuming for a good half minute holding those shears."

Lucas paused. Adele glanced up and caught him looking out at a memory only he could see. "What happened?" she asked.

He grunted. "Oh, he put those shears back. In my house we knew when it came to Mom's flowers her word was law. Thing is, when I was young, I would hear or watch my parents have those little arguments and think how stupid they were. It used to annoy the hell out of me. Now I understand. Life isn't perfect because people aren't perfect. And those arguments? That's just love having a disagreement. I'd give almost anything to walk back into my house and be able to listen to them arguing about those damn flowers again. Late at night, when it's real quiet and I can clear my head, I hear them sometimes, talking, laughing, or even singing. I never thought I would remember all those songs they used to sing. Every song. Every word."

Lucas's pain was palpable. Adele motioned with her thumb toward their vehicles parked back on the road. "You want to grab a bite?"

Lucas rubbed his nose, sniffed, and shook his head. "Nah. Not that I don't appreciate the offer. I do. I think I'm just going to head home and rest up."

Adele looked at him more closely, trying to better determine his mood. "Are you okay?"

He gazed out at the waters again. Adele noted how he had the same faraway look Roland did when taking in the very same view. He smiled and gave a half nod. His voice was stronger, more certain.

"Yeah, I'm good. I'm blessed to have the life I do and that I can count people like you as friends. Anyway, I'm gonna get going."

Lucas turned and began to make his way to his SUV. As she watched him go Adele wondered whether his outlook was in fact as positive as he would have her believe. He stopped halfway to his vehicle and turned around. His brow furrowed and his lips drew tightly together as if he wasn't certain he should say something. Adele waited, allowing him time to make up his mind.

"If anything happened between you and someone else, it's not my place to judge," he said. "We aren't dating. I don't want to lose a friend over jealousy I have no right to place on another. With my dad gone I have a lot of thinking to do. Pretty soon it'll be election time and maybe the voters decide they want to go a different direction as far as sheriff is concerned. Who knows? What I *do* know is that you've become a very important person in my life. Not just because you're cute as hell, either. You're damn smart and have a great heart. I respect you. I respect you enough to let you decide your own way in your own time. Maybe down the road you and I become something more. Maybe not. I'm fine with waiting to find out. I just wanted you to know that. You take care, Adele."

Lucas held up his hand and gave a little wave that was accompanied by a crooked half smile. Then he was inside his SUV and driving away, leaving Adele to try to absorb what he had just done for her. By saying what he did, Lucas relieved her of the guilt she had been holding onto for not telling him what had happened with Roland. Lucas may not have known the specifics, but he clearly suspected something took place and he wanted Adele to know he wouldn't judge her for it.

I respect you. I respect you enough to let you decide your own way on your own time.

It was a remarkable concession from a man Adele knew was rightfully proud of how he had chosen to live his life. They were words that deepened the stirrings of love she felt for him during the performance at his father's service. Whether or not she should tell him of those feelings remained unknown to her, which led her to believe it wasn't yet the right time. They both needed space to grow and mature and find their own way before they might possibly find each other.

Cattle Point's late-afternoon weather was unusually calm. The waters beyond the point had a smooth blue, glistening sheen. Seagulls called out from the beach below, arguing over scraps uncovered by the outgoing tide. Lucas was right. A new season, like the turning of a page, was emerging.

Adele closed her eyes, breathed that future in and held it, savoring the possibilities. Her life was truly her own.

She intended to live it.

EPILOGUE

Two weeks later

"Cheers." Tilda clinked her wine glass against Adele's. It was late evening inside the softly lit lobby of the Roche Harbor Hotel. No guests had checked in that day. Another cold spell, a final gasp of winter, had most likely kept them away. Even Phillip had already left his place behind the lobby desk to return home. Tilda had opened a bottle of her favorite Malbec to share with Adele.

"Did you finally read the screenplay?"

Adele nodded. Not only had she read the manuscript, she was mesmerized by it. The work left her just a bit jealous over the writing ability of the young Hollywood director and writer, Vincent Weber, who intended to turn her little newspaper article *The Writer* into a film of the same name.

"It was very good. To be honest I didn't want to like it and I still don't know how I feel about Brixton using Decklan and Calista's story as the vehicle for his own return to the world of the living. I don't want it to turn into some Hollywood sideshow."

"You're right to be cautious, Adele. Artists so often are selfishly demanding yet surprisingly fragile, requiring a great deal of maintenance. At this point, though, the proverbial horse is out of the barn, and I don't foresee the likelihood there will be any putting it back.

Brixton is determined to see the project through and is already coordinating his return with an army of publicists to guide that process along. I also spoke with Calista recently. Both she and Decklan have approved the film—for a sizeable bit of cash I might add. They intend to be back to the islands this spring. She asked that I tell you how much they are both looking forward to seeing you again."

Tilda took a sip of the dark-red wine and then tilted her head. "Besides, as you said, the screenplay *is* quite good. And don't sell yourself short. It was your article that was the genesis for its inspiration. Don't ever forget that."

Adele silently admitted to herself some part of her was looking forward to seeing *The Writer* on the big screen. "So, the director, this Vincent Weber, he's coming to the islands as well?"

Tilda nodded. "Yes. He should be here at the same time as Decklan and Calista. He wants to meet them in person, discuss his vision for the film, and then, according to Calista, start scouting locations on the islands. The hope is to begin filming by summer. It's going to be rather exciting and with Brixton's unexpected involvement, likely to attract a considerable amount of attention given so many still believe he's actually dead."

"I imagine for local hotel owners, all of those people coming to the islands to work and watch will be very good for business. It should be quite a summer season."

Tilda held up her glass and grinned. "Indeed." She put her glass back down. "Speaking of which, I have a small favor to ask. Could you please make sure this gets to the Workman family?" She slid a check across the table toward Adele. The amount was for $20,000. Word of the Workman family's struggle to pay for their daughter's medical care had finally spread beyond the tiny borders of Olga, and the people of the San Juan Islands had responded almost immediately with an outpouring of generosity. Tilda now wished to do the same.

"Oh, Tilda, you don't have to do that. It's too much."

Tilda shook her head while clicking her tongue against the roof of her mouth. "Your friend Mr. Soros is not the only person of means around here. I've done quite well for myself over these many years. That money will help a family in need. I haven't done enough to give back. It's about time I started."

"Okay, I'll see they get it. It's a wonderful gesture."

The hotel's entrance door opened, bringing with it a rush of cold air that poured into the lobby. Both women turned to look, believing it was Phillip having returned after forgetting something.

It wasn't Phillip.

Sergei Kozlov closed the door behind him. The Russian's face was badly bruised, his lip swollen, and a red gash dissected the bridge of his nose. With his head lowered, he looked back at the women, his dark eyes glowering from underneath heavy lids. He swayed from side to side. The stench of alcohol rose up from him and settled over the table Tilda and Adele remained sitting at.

He slowly lifted an arm and pointed at Adele. His heavily accented voice was a slurred sandpaper growl. "I knew you were trouble from the first time I saw you talking with Roland. A nosey bitch is what you are. Look at my face. This is the trouble you brought to me. I know it was you who put the idea into Roland's head to give Cattle Point away to the county, you and your ideas and your newspaper stories. Yuri punished me but don't think he is not considering your punishment as well. He forgets nothing and forgives less. What will it take for you to learn to keep your mouth shut? You think you know everything? Like who left that book of matches on your boat? Hmmm? You think that was me? Ah, see? You *don't* know everything, do you? How will you like it when I make your face look like mine?"

Tilda was first to stand up. Her long blue dress nearly touched the floor, making it appear like she was gliding rather than walking as she crossed the lobby to confront Sergei, her red hair hanging over her shoulders and down her back. He scowled, confused by her seeming lack of fear. She was nearly as tall as him as her eyes bored into his.

"Sit back down old woman before I—"

Tilda's open hand launched like a striking cobra and descended. Her palm whipped across the Russian's face, snapping his head to the side. Sergei's eyes went wide. He stepped back, appearing bewildered, angry, and even fearful of Tilda's stern-faced glare.

"I don't know you, but I know of you," she hissed. "This is my hotel—my home. You are not a guest. You have not been invited. And you will leave now."

Sergei's slowly traced the red mark on his face. He clenched a fist, his courage partially returned as he began to snarl a rebuke. "You crazy old bitch. I am going to—"

Again, Tilda slapped him. The second blow was delivered even more powerfully than the first, the crack of skin against her palm echoing throughout the lobby. "Go. Return to wherever it is you're from, and don't ever come back here."

Sergei's mouth started to open. Tilda's eyes flared as she prepared to strike him yet again. The Russian's mouth snapped shut. He took one unsteady step back and then another, until his shoulders were pressed against the door. His eyes darted toward Adele, who had by then crossed the lobby to stand next to Tilda.

Tilda pointed at Sergei. "Don't look at her. Don't say another word. Just turn around, open that door, and be on your way."

It was then that Adele saw Sergei for what he had become. Or perhaps it was what he had always been: a beaten and broken creature, afraid and desperate. *Which might make him even more dangerous.*

"I would do what she says, Sergei," Adele said. "I've already messaged the sheriff."

Sergei lifted a trembling hand and wiped at the corners of his mouth. His other hand reached behind him to grasp the door handle. The Russian did as he was told. He turned around, opened the door, and left.

"Did you really message the sheriff?" Tilda asked.

Adele looked up at Tilda and shook her head. "No. I don't even have my phone with me."

Tilda tipped her head. "Well played."

After locking the door, both women returned to the table where a final glass of wine awaited them.

Adele slowly swirled the contents of her glass for a moment and then looked up. "Why weren't you afraid of Sergei?"

Tilda straightened in her chair while folding her arms across her chest. "I *was* afraid of him. I simply chose not to allow him to see it. I learned long ago that the true power of a bully is the fear they create in others. They feed off it. It emboldens them. Remove that fear, and they starve. They go away in search of more accommodating victims."

Adele's features tightened. "I wish I could be that strong."

"You *are* that strong. You just don't realize it yet. Life at its best remains an often-difficult thing, and for a woman even more so. We are the sisterhood of misfortunes, scrabbling for our place in a world of men with large egos and too little sense. I see your potential, Adele. I sit here now before you, and it takes my breath away when I consider the magnitude of that potential. I consider it, and I envy it."

Tilda took hold of her glass and held it high over the table. "Tell me, what would you have done if Sergei had not backed down? What if he had instead chosen to fight back against me?"

Adele stared down at the table as she pondered the question. In her mind she replayed the moment she saw Sergei's fist clench, thinking then he intended to strike Tilda with it. Adele's gaze lifted. Tilda still held her glass over the table as she awaited the answer.

Adele grabbed hold of her own glass and raised it. Her voice was low and her response as succinct as it was confident. "I would have kicked his ass."

The sound the two glasses made as they lightly touched reminded Adele of the tolling of a bell—a declaration of the considerable potential Tilda hoped to see Adele more fully realize. Tilda brought the glass to her lips, flung her head back, and emptied its contents in a single swallow. After setting the glass on the table, she looked at Adele and nodded.

"Of that I have no doubt, my dear—no doubt at all."

With one bottle emptied, another was opened, just as a moment in a life is soon replaced by the next. Midnight came and went as Adele and Tilda drank, talked, and laughed, their bond growing stronger in the process.

One was young. One was less so. Both were equally grateful to be in the company of a true friend.

We should all be so lucky.

Did you enjoy the story? Your feedback is important. Please take a moment to leave a review for *Murder on Matia* on its Amazon book page. Thank you! —DWU

ABOUT THE AUTHOR

D.W. Ulsterman lives in the Pacific Northwest with his beautiful wife of 24 years. They are the proud parents of two grown children and friends to Mattie the Cat and Dublin the Dobe.

When not writing he can often be found navigating the waters of his beloved San Juan Islands. His most popular works include *The Irish Cowboy* and *The San Juan Islands Mystery* series.

All of his novels can be purchased via his Amazon author page.

For direct inquiries you can email him at: dwulsterman@gmail.com

CPSIA information can be obtained
at www.ICGtesting.com
Printed in the USA
LVHW081545300523
748293LV00010B/928